A Sack Full of Dollars

John Smiley is a travelling entertainer. As he and his son and daughter are approaching the small township of Silver Spur in Kansas, they encounter Black Bart, a notorious gunman, who demands money and carbine-whips Smiley's son. Smiley, however, is a skilled boxer and humiliates the outlaw, leaving Black Bart hell bent on revenge, leading to a series of dark and bloody events when the family reach their destination.

A Sack Full of Dollars

Lee Lejeune

A Black Horse Western

ROBERT HALE

© Lee Lejeune 2017
First published in Great Britain 2017

ISBN 978-0-7198-2467-8

The Crowood Press
The Stable Block
Crowood Lane
Ramsbury
Marlborough
Wiltshire SN8 2HR

www.bhwesterns.com

Robert Hale is an imprint
of The Crowood Press

The right of Lee Lejeune to be identified as
author of this work has been asserted by him
in accordance with the Copyright, Designs and
Patents Act 1988

Typeset by
Derek Doyle & Associates, Shaw Heath
Printed and bound in Great Britain by
CPI Group (UK) Ltd, Croydon, CR0 4YY

CHAPTER ONE

His name was John Smiley, and when he was on the road he said to his audiences, 'Cry with John and smile with Smiley!' which usually made them chuckle. John was an entertainer. He told jokes, sang folksongs, performed one-man plays, strummed on his banjo, and even did a few card tricks. He was well known in Kansas but never stayed in one township for more than a few days – he just kept moving on, always eager to explore new territory and find new audiences.

You could say he was a failed musician and a failed actor. Some might have said he was just a travelling bum or a ham entertainer who was too lazy to settle down and do any *real* work. But John didn't take account of such talk; he just moved on from one location to the next, laughing and singing and telling jokes, some of them in extremely bad taste.

That was all right if a man was on his own. The trouble was, John had a family and most of the time they were on the road with him. So what about school? Well, to give John full credit, he had taught both his son and his daughter to read and write, and they were pretty bright kids. In the early days John had been trained as a teacher, but he

5

couldn't abide the sedentary life, nor the school kids who didn't give a damn about book learning.

His own kids were now fully grown: Katie was eighteen and John Junior was a couple of years younger. What about John's wife? you might ask. Well, she had died some years earlier of consumption – or perhaps a broken heart!

In his early years John had been something of a charmer. Some might have said he could charm the birds off the trees. That's how he had charmed Sarah into marrying him – but that was before she knew he was a bum who would never settle down to a normal life.

On this particular day he and his son and daughter were on the road to a place called Silver Spur where they might stay for up to a week, depending on how well the performances were received. John knew Silver Spur well and the people appreciated his act. He had rehearsed a couple of new plays, and even one speech from the great Shakespeare himself which he thought might please the people of Silver Spur. After all, they didn't get much honest entertainment, did they?

John was actually running through his lines when his daughter Katie interrupted him.

'Pa, I see riders and they're coming towards us.'

John looked along the trail and saw for himself. There were three riders and they were heading straight towards them. Nothing unusual about that, except that these men were armed to the teeth! John tightened his jaw and got ready to whip up his team, but the three riders were right across the trail and one of them held up his hand' 'D'you mind pulling up!' the man said, and it wasn't so much a request as a command.

'Are they lawmen?' John Junior asked his pa.

John Senior didn't reply. There was no time, anyway.

The other two riders rode right up to the rig.

Katie, who was sitting next to her pa in the driving seat, said between her teeth, 'Pa, I don't like the look of this.'

John Smiley didn't say a thing and he wasn't smiling either. He just nodded and looked at the leading man who was holding a Winchester carbine pointing towards them.

'You mind just stepping down!' the man ordered. He was a heavy-set *hombre* with a well bearded face, and his voice sounded like gravel shaken in a pan.

John Smiley attempted to smile. 'What do you want with us, sir?'

Katie thought his voice sounded sort of unnaturally high, like someone singing treble in a choir, which worried her.

One of the other riders laughed. And the leader said, 'We want what you've got, sir, every last dollar of it.' And he laughed too, somewhat less pleasantly.

'Well, we ain't got much to offer you,' John Junior piped up. 'We're just travelling entertainers and we don't carry much stock.'

Katie thought that was real brave of her brother considering he was only sixteen with just a few hairs sprouting from his chin.

'So you don't carry much stock,' the man jeered and he seized young John by the arm and pulled him down from his perch. Poor John Junior fell on the hard dusty trail and lay still. Katie held back a scream because she sensed it might make matters a whole lot worse.

The leader switched his attention to her. 'Well, now, young lady, and who might you be?'

'I'm Katie Smiley,' she said with scarcely a tremor, 'and like my brother said, we're just travellers going about our own business.'

7

'Well, now,' the bearded man said. 'That's well spoken, lady. You got a lot of grit and I admire a girl with grit, don't I, boys?'

'You sure do, Bart,' the other two laughed.

'OK,' the bearded man said. 'Perhaps you'll be kind enough to step right down and we'll see what we can find, shall we?'

Katie looked at her father and he shook his head. Then they both climbed down from the rig.

The bearded man's sidekicks were looking over the two horses somewhat critically.

The bearded man motioned with his carbine. 'Just stand over there at the side of the trail while we take a looksee.'

John Smiley touched his daughter's arm reassuringly and they both went to the side of the trail. John Junior dragged himself to his feet and shook his head. He was obviously dazed from his fall.

'That's no way to treat a man,' he said to the bearded *hombre.*

The bearded man gave a nasty grin. 'You call yourself a man?' he sneered. And raised his carbine and struck the youth across the side of the head.

John Junior dropped like a stone and blood poured from his head. Katie screamed and John Smiley looked down at John Junior with horror. 'That's my boy!' he said.

'Then you should have teached him to be more respectful to his elders and betters,' the man said.

'Why did you do that?' Katie demanded. Then she got down on her knees and cradled her brother's head in her arms. He's still breathing, she thought. She looked up at the bearded man. 'You're a brute!' she shouted, 'nothing but a brute pretending to be a man.'

8

A faint look of surprise crossed the man's face, but then he gave a neighing laugh, and the other two laughed as well.

John Junior groaned and Katie and her father helped him to his feet. Now John Smiley's eyes were blazing. 'You hurt my boy!' he shouted, 'and I won't forget that.'

The bearded man looked slightly nonplussed. 'What you gonna do about it, Pansy Man?'

'You get down off that horse of yours and hand your gun over and I'll show you what I'm going to do about it.' Among other things, John Smiley had learned to box. In fact, he'd once given boxing lessons in a circus ring.

The bearded man laughed. 'Are you challenging me to play fisticuffs with you, Pansy Man?'

'If you put aside that carbine and take off your gunbelt I'll show you what a real man can do,' John Smiley challenged.

The bearded man grinned and turned to his sidekicks. 'What do you think, boys? Shall I teach this pansy man a lesson or two?'

'You bet,' one of his sidekicks said.

'Make it two or three,' the other sidekick jeered, 'looks like he could do with a lesson in good manners.'

The bearded man got down from his horse and handed his carbine to the first sidekick. Then he unbuckled his gunbelt and handed it to the other man. 'Take care of this, Mart,' he said. 'Take care of it till I teach this apology for a man a lesson he'll never forget.'

'You bet, Bart,' the sidekick said again.

The bearded man was heavy and tall, six feet or more in height and broad as a barn door.

'Don't do it, Pa,' Katie said to her father. 'The man will kill you.'

But there was no stopping John Smiley now. 'Better to die fighting than to play the coward,' he said to her. He stepped forward on to the trail and waited with his fists clenched and his arms hanging by his sides. Katie saw that her father was at least six inches shorter and a good deal less heavy than the bearded man and he looked like a dwarf beside him. It was a matter of David and Goliath, only John Smiley didn't have a sling or a pebble: he just had his two bare fists.

The bearded man laughed and waded forwards and struck out with a fist as large and hard as a boulder. But the fist never connected. John Smiley ducked adroitly and stepped aside and the bearded man missed by inches and staggered sideways, off balance. Then something amazing occurred. John Smiley suddenly sprang to life, and he struck out so quickly his fists seemed to blur. And they made contact, too. There was a thump! thump! thump! as his fists burrowed into the big man's body. Then as Bart the Beard doubled up and fell, John Smiley's foot came down on his ample belly with a sharp jerk.

The two sidekicks looked down in amazement as the bearded man lay flat on his back wheezing like an asphyxiated goat.

'Well, I'll be damned!' the man called Mart exclaimed.

The bearded man rolled over and tried to struggle to his feet, but John Smiley was now in total control and he stepped in and kicked the bearded man right in the middle of his ugly face. The bearded man fell with a thump on to his back again and blood spurted from his nose.

John Smiley was so enraged he could hardly speak, but be held out his fists to the two sidekicks. 'Who's next?' he shouted. 'One at a time! Come on!' And now, despite his bloody head, John Junior rose and stood beside his father with his fists held ready.

But Mart and the other sidekick had other ideas. Instead of holding up their fists they drew their shooters and levelled them at John Smiley and his children.

'I don't take no boxing lessons from you,' the man called Mart exclaimed. 'You come one step closer and I'll blow your head right off your shoulders.'

Now Bart, the bearded man, was on his knees. He hoisted himself up on to his feet and wiped the blood off his nose with the back of his hand. 'Give me my gunbelt,' he said, stretching out his hand towards Mart. Mart handed Bart the gunbelt and Bart strapped it round his waist. Then he drew his Colt 44 and cocked it. 'Now', he snarled at John Smiley, 'I'm gonna shoot you down like a rabid cur right in front of your two kids, you know that?' He took a step forwards, 'But first of all I'm gonna shoot you where you'll feel it most. Then I'm gonna shoot you right between your damned stupid eyes. Then we're gonna burn your rig right down to the ground, but you won't give a damn because you'll be stone dead. Do you hear me?'

'I hear you,' John Smiley said.

Then John Smiley Junior spoke up bravely. 'If you kill my pa you'll have to kill me first.'

'And me,' Katie said, stepping in front of John Smiley.

The bearded man wagged his head from side to side. 'The whole family, eh,' he said. 'Well, if that's the way it has to be, that's the way it has to be.' He raised the Colt and held it out straight level with his shoulder.

Keep him talking, John Smiley thought. Give the brute time to cool off and think again. 'Consider the consequences, man. You kill three members of a family and

11

you'll end up swinging by the neck from the gallows tree.'
He turned to the two henchmen.

'And you'll be swinging with him, you know that!'

'You think so?' Black Bart snarled.

'I know so,' John Smiley said.

Black Bart glanced at his two henchmen and grinned.
'What do you say, boys? Shall we just shoot the pa and free
the kids? Or better still, maybe we should hold the girl in
case they come looking for us, eh?'

Katie noticed that the two henchmen looked a little
uneasy as the picture of the gallows swam before their
eyes. She felt her pa tense beside her, and she spoke up.
'You think it's worth swinging on that tree for what we've
got, Mart?'

The man called Mart gave a start. 'Who are you calling
Mart?' he said.

'That's your name, isn't it?'

'Are you a witch or something?'

Katie knew how to take the initiative: she'd been in the
entertainment business with her father long enough to tell
a hawk from a hand saw. 'Let me tell you this, Mister,' she
said, 'I have powers that you and your partner never
dreamt of.' She stared directly at the man called Mart and
he seemed to turn a shade paler than old parchment.

'There ain't no such thing,' he said, but his voice
betrayed him, and Katie saw that he was terrified of the
invisible powers.

'Listen, Bart,' the other henchman said. 'There's
nothing here for us. These folk don't have more than a
two-bit piece between them.'

But Black Bart wasn't so easily deterred. 'Maybe there's
witchcraft involved here,' he said in his gravelly tone, 'but
I'm holding the ace card here in the shape of this Colt

revolver, and it never let me down so far.'

'So far's a long stretch,' John Junior piped up. 'And at the end of that long stretch you'll be as dead as a cold pork chop.'

Black Bart wasn't blessed with a great sense of humour. The next second he brought his Colt revolver down level and fired a shot. John Junior gave an involuntary hop as the bullet struck the trail, but nobody fell. 'That's my magical firestick!' Black Bart boasted. 'I ain't never seen anything stronger, you hear me!' And he fired another shot. 'Set fire to the rig!' he shouted at his two henchmen.

'What about the horses?' Mart said.

'OK, unhitch the horses, and we take them with us!' Black Bart roared.

But before they could move the other man said, 'Listen up, boys. I hear riders coming.'

Black Bart paused to listen. 'OK, boys, let's vamoose.'

The three mounted up quickly.

'See you in hell,' Black Bart said. He fired a shot in the air and they rode off hell for leather.

John Smiley sat down on the side of the trail and wondered just what had hit him. His daughter Katie was examining her brother's wounds. He had a deep cut on the side of his head where the barrel of Black Bart's carbine had struck him, but he was fully conscious and furiously angry.

Before any of them could speak, they heard the sound of galloping horses drawing closer and two riders appeared. One of them threw up his arm and they drew to a halt. He looked at the rig and then at the three figures sitting at the side of the trail.

'Are you guys OK?' he asked in a deep and friendly

sounding tone. 'We heard shots and thought you might be in trouble.'

'We were indeed in trouble,' John Smiley said. 'Three *hombres* stopped us and threatened to shoot us. Luckily you came along in time.'

The man with the pleasant-sounding voice dismounted. 'Don't I know you, Mister?'

'The name's Smiley,' John Smiley said, getting to his feet and holding out his hand.

'Sure,' the man said. 'I've seen your show.' He got down from his horse and peered at John Smiley Junior. 'Did those scumbags do that to you?' he asked.

'Pistol whipped him with a Winchester carbine,' John Smiley said.

'That head wound looks pretty bad to me. Who did that to you?'

'Man called Bart. He had a big black beard.'

'Black Bart,' the man said. 'You're lucky you're still alive, young man.'

'If you hadn't come when you did, we might all be lying on the trail stiff and dead,' John Smiley said. 'So we must thank you, sir.'

'Don't mention it,' the man said in his pleasant sounding tone. 'The name's Adam Kirk. Most people call me Kirk.'

'Well, thank you, Kirk.' John Smiley pressed Kirk's hand, and Kirk had a good firm grip.

'So where are you headed, John Smiley?' Kirk asked him.

'We're on our way to Silver Spur,' John Smiley said. 'Got an *amigo* up there called Kev Stanley, runs the Long Branch Saloon.'

Kirk nodded. 'I know the man well. Stayed in the Long Branch once or twice. So you're doing a show up there?'

'That's the idea. Kev's awful keen on theatricals and stuff.

14

We usually get a good reception in Silver Spur. No more than peanuts but it keeps us on the road.'

'That's what life's about, my friend.' Kirk turned to the other man. 'Charlie, you're the medic around here. Look at this young fella's wound and fix him up, will you?'

'I sure will,' Charlie got down from his horse and reached for his medical kit.

'Useful to have a qualified medic by your side,' Kirk said. 'Charlie almost managed to qualify but he quit medical school because he couldn't stand the sight of blood. Isn't that so, Charlie?'

Charlie nodded. 'Can't abide the sight of dead men, either. Makes me feel real creepy all over.' He knelt down and started examining John Junior's wound. 'Needs stitching up,' he said. 'Otherwise you're going to have a big scar on the side of your bean like a second mouth. You could tell folk it's a duelling scar. They say the gells in Germany go for duelling scars in a really big way, but I wouldn't recommend it too highly. So why don't you just lie back here and I'll do the business as best I can.'

John Junior lay back on the side of the trail and Charlie the Medic stitched him up in almost no time at all. It was painful but John Junior clenched his teeth and bore it stoically like a man. Charlie had no antiseptic but he figured whiskey would do just as well and he was really generous with the supply. 'No ordinary hooch this,' he claimed. 'Guaranteed to kill off every germ in the alphabet, that's for sure.' Then he plied the curved needle with great precision, just like a top notch surgeon.

Katie hated to watch her brother suffering but she was curious about the men who had ridden up and saved them. She noted they were armed but they seemed friendly enough. She was particularly drawn to Adam Kirk, who was maybe twenty-five or twenty-six. He was tall, though not as tall as the bully Black Bart. He also looked muscular and strong. But it was the glint in his eyes that attracted her most. When he looked around, he seemed to take in everything at a glance. And at that moment he was looking at her.

'Are you part of the show?' he asked her.

She nodded and felt the blood rising to her face. 'I help,' she said modestly. 'My pa and my brother do most of the real work. But I play piano, and cook and keep the accounts mostly.'

'Well, that's a useful part of any outfit,' Kirk said. 'Charlie can't fry an egg without turning it bad. And when it comes to keeping books we might as well be on the moon. Luckily we don't have any books to keep.'

Charlie the Medic gave a quiet laugh.

'Where are you boys headed?' John Smiley asked him.

'General direction of Silver Spur,' Kirk told him. 'You can call it an armed escort if you like. Just in case Black Bart shows up again.'

'So you know Black Bart?' John Smiley asked him.

Kirk grinned. 'We've crossed swords a few times but I don't care too much for him. I know him more by reputation than personal acquaintance. I think you could say you've had a narrow escape. That *hombre* would shoot you down as well as saying good day to you, sir. I heard his ma was frightened by a grizzly before he was born. Or maybe he's the son of a grizzly himself. Who can tell?'

John Smiley, John Junior and Katie got back on the wagon and the party rode on. Kirk rode beside the wagon on Katie's side.

'You been on the road long?' he asked her.

'Since I was a kid,' she said.

16

'So you never went to school?'

'There was no time for school. My ma and pa taught me all I know.' She told Kirk about the loss of her mother. He was easy to talk to, the kind of man you found yourself trusting immediately; he might have been a brother or a close relation. As she spoke he kept looking at her and smiling and nodding with empathy.

'We do have a place some way east of here,' she told him, 'but we hardly ever stay there, except in winter. My aunt keeps it in order.'

'Well, I guess every man and woman needs somewhere to lay his head.'

Katie wanted to ask him why he and Charlie were on the trail and why they were armed, but she decided to leave her questions unsaid for the present.

When they reached the outskirts of Silver Spur, Adam Kirk said to John Smiley, 'Well, sir, I'm real glad we met, but this is where we part company, I guess.'

'So, you're not stopping off at Silver Spur?' John Smiley said.

'No, sir,' Kirk replied. 'I'm afraid we have other things boiling in the pot. So we have to move right along.'

Charlie the Medic chuckled. 'Yeah, we have to roll on,' he said. 'But give our regards to Kev Stanley and tell him we'll look in on him later. And if you happen to see Sheriff Kincade, give him our best wishes, too.

'We'll do that, Charlie,' John Smiley assured him.

'And thanks for mending my head,' John Smiley Junior said to Charlie the Medic.

'That was a real pleasure,' Charlie said. 'You were the grittiest patient I've had in years. Keep that wound clean and visit the sawbones as soon as you can.'

Kirk and Charlie raised their hands and rode off just as

the trail turned towards Silver Spur, and John Smiley and his son and daughter went on into the township.

Katie wondered what had hit her, but she wasn't thinking of Black Bart or Charlie: she was thinking of that good-looking young man, Adam Kirk.

CHAPTER TWO

Kev Stanley appeared at the doors of the Long Branch Saloon as soon as the rig pulled in. It was late afternoon, and there weren't many customers in the saloon apart from Tiny Broadhurst who spent most of his days and half the night propping up the bar. Tiny Broadhurst was a mountain of a man but as soft and wobbly as a kid's jelly. He liked to boast, mostly about how he had won the recent war almost single-handed. Kev tolerated Tiny because he felt sorry for him, and Tiny played on it to the full. Sophia Stanley, Kev's wife, wasn't quite as sympathetic. She regarded Tiny Broadhurst as a pain in the butt and a parasite on the backside of society!

Kev Stanley walked across the sidewalk just as John Smiley jumped down from the rig. 'Good to see you, John,' Kev greeted. 'I'm real glad you got here. My, how you two have grown!' he marvelled, looking with admiration at the brother and sister. 'What happened to your head?' he asked John Junior.

'It had a disagreement with a Winchester carbine,' John Smiley told him.

'How come?' Kev asked.

John Smiley explained and John Junior looked embarrassed. He could feel his head throbbing under the bandage. It was even more painful than earlier.

'So you met Black Bart and his gang?' Kev said.

'There were only two of them apart from Black Bart,' Katie piped up. 'One was called Mart. They all looked like they'd taken supper with the Devil himself.'

Kev looked puzzled. 'Can't think why they would hold up you and your rig,' he said, 'After all, and with all respect, you aren't exactly rich pickings, are you?'

'We'd have been a lot poorer pickings if they'd burned the rig!' John Smiley said angrily. 'Lucky a guy called Kirk and his friend Charlie the Medic rode in like the Fifth Cavalry in time to save us from being shot to death!'

Kev stared at him in amazement. 'You mean Adam Kirk?'

'That's what he called himself,' John Smiley said. 'Told me he knew you and he'd seen some of our shows.'

Kev Stanley grinned. 'Sure, we've met. Well now, why don't you park your rig at the back next to the barn and come right in for refreshments? Sophia will be real glad to see you.'

After they had parked the rig, John Smiley and the family went through to the bar where Tiny Broadhurst was yacking away about how he had won the Battle of Gettysburg single handed to everyone within hearing distance. 'So I ran out right in the face of the enemy,' he croaked in a strangely high-pitched voice. 'I don't rightly know how I got away with my life but I did! I guess they were too amazed to shoot straight!' And he guffawed loudly at his own joke.

'You must have been a really big target too!' someone shouted from the other end of the bar.

20

Tiny paused and turned in time to see John Smiley and the two young ones disappearing into the back room.

'Why, John Smiley!' he shouted. 'Good to see you, man! When's the show?'

In fact there was a notice for the John Smiley show pinned to the noticeboard right above his head but he was too busy yacking away about his heroic deeds to notice it.

Kev's wife Sophia had a really nice meal prepared for the family. She was no Thespian lover herself, but the John Smiley show attracted a lot of customers, and that was good for business. 'Who gave you that bump on the head?' she asked John Junior.

'It's nothing,' he said. 'Charlie the Medic fixed it.'

'So you met Charlie the Medic?'

'Sure did,' John Smiley responded. 'Kirk said he dropped out of medical school. But he sure knew his business.'

'So you met Kirk as well?' she asked sharply.

John Junior was in no position to reply. At that moment he got up from the table and held his hand to his mouth and then lurched towards the door. Katie ran out after him and they heard him retching and vomiting somewhere off stage as his father would have put it.

'That boy is sick,' Sophia announced somewhat superfluously. 'Kevin, go down and see whether Doc Buchanan is busy at the moment!'

Kev Stanley opened his arms in astonishment. 'What, right now?'

'Right now!' she demanded. 'Didn't you see the colour of that poor boy's face? I think he's got a concussion or something!'

Kev Stanley pulled a face at John Smiley and went right out through the bar where Tiny Broadhurst was holding

21

up his glass for another drink.

When Doc Buchanan showed up in the saloon, John Smiley Junior was lying semiconscious on a bed. The doc examined the wound and prescribed a sedative. 'This young man needs rest,' he said. 'That dint on the skull could have knocked him clean out of this world into the next. There might be internal bleeding. He needs rest and loving care. Can you provide that, Mrs Stanley?'

Like many good women who had seen a lot of the world, Sophia Stanley was tough as saddle leather on the outside but soft as custard on the inside. 'Don't you worry, Doctor. The boy can rest up here just as long as he needs to.'

Doc Buchanan grinned. 'I'll look in early tomorrow morning, and if you need me, you know where to find me.'

John Smiley was deeply concerned: he'd never seen John Junior looking so sick before. The boy's face had turned a sort of cheese green colour, and when he tried to speak it came out in an incoherent babble. Katie sat beside her brother's bed and tried to hold his hand, but the boy became restless and feverish, and he lashed out wildly. Then he shuddered and lapsed into a semi-coma.

Sophia Stanley looked down at the boy and frowned. 'This boy is seriously ill,' she said. She turned to her husband. 'Get Doc Buchanan back here right now,' she said. 'Tell him the patient has taken a turn for the worst and needs attention immediately, not tomorrow morning. Tomorrow morning might be too late!'

Kev Stanley didn't pull a face at anyone this time. He just opened the door and ran down Main Street to the doctor's office.

Doc Buchanan and his wife were enjoying a good night drink when Kev arrived.

'The boy's taken a turn for the worst!' Kev gasped. 'Can you come right now?'

Doc Buchanan might not have been the best doctor in the Western United States but he was pretty quick when it came to emergencies. So he grabbed his medical bag and looked at his wife Suzanne. 'You'd better come with me, Sue. This might be a case of life and death.' Though he spoke without emotion, the message was quite clear: John Smiley Junior was at death's door!

In the room behind the Long Branch Saloon the candles and oil lamps burned all night as Doc Buchanan and his wife Suzanne fought to save John Junior's life. As soon as Martin Buchanan saw the patient he realized there had been internal bleeding in the boy's skull and there was only one thing to do; he needed to make an incision in the skull and release the blood! So he gave the boy enough chloroform to put him to sleep and then got to work. It would be a tricky operation, but with Suzanne's help he could do it.

Katie Smiley refused to leave her brother. So Suzanne enlisted her help and Katie fought bravely as one of the team. And Sophia did what she could do to help, which wasn't much.

John Smiley sat with Kev Stanley in the bar-room. Kev had given his friend a stiff drink but John Smiley left it untouched. They sat for a couple of hours without saying much. John Smiley was listening to every creak and groan in the old timbers as though they might have significance.

'What's happening?' he said to himself. 'What in hell's name is going on?'

Kev Stanley didn't know how to answer. Though he was kind and resourceful in most emergencies, he felt quite powerless in this situation.

'Do you pray?' John Smiley asked him suddenly.

Kev raised his head and looked at John Smiley in surprise. The poor man had the expression of a beaten dog and Kev didn't know how to reply. He'd been brought up to pray but he hadn't said a prayer since he was in short pants. So he said, 'I was brought up to say my prayers but I haven't had a lot of time lately.'

'Do you think anyone listens?' John Smiley asked him.

That was one hell of a question. Kev Stanley shook his head. 'You mean like a man up there?' he asked.

'I guess so,' John Smiley said.

Kev Stanley shook his head again. 'Well, John,' he said, 'we'd have to ask the padre about that. They tell me he's a good man and he knows the answers to most questions.'

They were still looking at one another when the door opened and Doc Buchanan's wife Suzanne stood there and she wasn't smiling.

John Smiley got to his feet slowly and said, 'Well?'

Suzanne shook her head and said, 'I'm sorry, John.'

John Smiley swayed back as though he'd been struck by a stone in the middle of his forehead. 'What? You mean. . . ?' He didn't complete the sentence.

Suzanne nodded. 'He went five minutes back.'

John Smiley looked at her aghast. Then his knees buckled and he sank down at the table and put his head in his hands. 'My God,' he said, 'this is isn't true. Tell me it isn't true.'

But it was true, and everyone knew it. John Smiley Junior had suffered a brain haemorrhage that had killed him. John Smiley and Katie were devastated. John Smiley

Junior had been a strong, healthy young man with every-thing before him, and now he was lying dead in the back room of the Long Branch Saloon. Nobody knew what to say.

Doctor Martin Buchanan was devastated too.

'I should have realized immediately,' he said. 'If I'd operated earlier that poor kid might still be alive.'

'We did our best, Martin,' Suzanne said, 'And nobody can do better than that. What we have to do now is comfort that poor man. The girl too. She's a brave girl but she's lost her brother. You'd best go home and sleep now.'

Sleep was the last thing on Doc Buchanan's mind. He knew that a doctor must do his best, but not become too emotionally involved with his patients. That was easy enough to say, but not always so easy to do.

Katie was already with her pa, doing her best to comfort him.

'What are we going to do?' he asked. The loss of his wife had been bad enough, but now this. 'Is there a curse on me?' he asked his daughter.

'No, Pa,' she said. 'It's just bad luck we met those vicious men on the trail. John was brave, and he paid for it with his life.'

Doc Buchanan had given John Smiley a sedative, and after an hour he passed out.

Katie refused to take anything. She just sat in the saloon and talked to Sophia until the light of dawn began to slant between the roofs of Silver Spur.

Come sun-up, Doc Buchanan and his wife Suzanne were eating their breakfast in the room behind the doc's office. 'What d'you think we should do?' the doc asked his wife.

'Well, I'm going right back to Sophia and Kev and see

if I can do anything to help.'

That sounded like a good idea. Doc Buchanan thought he'd step over to see his friend Sheriff Jack Kincade. The two men had been friends ever since they came to Silver Spur, and whenever there was a problem they would meet and try to sort things out.

Doc Buchanan stepped out and looked towards the rising sun, and thought that life was good after all. He walked across Main Street and into Bridget's Diner where the Kincade family would be eating their breakfast. Jack Kincade had seen him through the window and he was already at the door to meet him. His two kids were inside getting ready for school, and Bridget Kincade was thinking about her menu for the day.

'Good morning, my friend,' Jack Kincade greeted him, holding out his hand.

Doc Buchanan grasped the hand and felt its strength, and it gave him a feeling of reassurance. The two friends always greeted one another with a shake of the hand even though they lived practically opposite one another on Main Street.

'I heard what happened yesterday,' Jack Kincade said. 'It was a bad business.'

Doc Buchanan filled him in on the details, and Jack Kincade nodded. 'I remember the boy. He must have been no older than Gregory.' Gregory was the sheriff's son, bright as a shiny button, just like John Smiley Junior. 'So you say they met Black Bart and Bart whipped the boy on the head with a Winchester carbine. That was a brutal thing to do to anyone, let alone a young boy.'

They walked over to the sheriff's office where the town drunk lay snoring in one of the cells. Jack Kincade unlocked the door and the prisoner snored on.

'Get yourself up off your butt and on to your two back feet' Jack said none too gently to the recumbent form. The prisoner opened one eye and groaned. 'Is it morning?' he asked in a whining tone.

'It's long past visiting time, my friend.' The sheriff gave him a prod on the backside. 'Get on your feet and get yourself out into the deep blue yonder and thank the good Lord you got a free bed for the night.'

The town drunk got himself up and blinked around like a sick dog. 'Do I get breakfast?' he asked.

Jack Kincade shook his head. 'You took in your supper and breakfast last night in liquid form. So get your arse home and tell your wife you're real sorry you spent all the dollars on that long liquid breakfast that you're about to bring up.' Then he opened the door and gave the drunk a push to help him on his way.

When he looked towards the Long Branch Saloon he saw a familiar figure walking towards him. It was John Smiley, the entertainer, and Smiley wasn't smiling. Jack knew Smiley passing well. He'd seen his shows from time to time and he reckoned Smiley was not only a class entertainer but a good man.

'Good morning, Mr Smiley,' Jack said quietly. 'I don't need to tell you how sorry I am about your loss.'

John Smiley nodded grimly. He seemed to have changed character completely. 'Thank you, Sheriff,' he said. 'Mind if I step into the jail house for a moment? There's something I'd like to say to you.'

'Well, of course, Mr Smiley. I was just talking to Doc Buchanan about what happened.'

John Smiley nodded and they both went into the jail house where Doc Buchanan was standing facing the door. John Smiley looked at the doctor and shook his head. 'You don't need to say anything, Doc. You did your best to save that boy but it wasn't to be.'

'He was a great kid,' Doc Buchanan said.

'He was the greatest,' the entertainer replied. He looked at the sheriff. 'What do you have on that guy with the black beard?'

'You mean Black Bart?' the sheriff asked.

'I mean the guy who killed my boy,' John Smiley said.

Jack Kincade gave a reluctant nod. 'He's up on the wall right there. Maybe you'd care to take a look.'

John Smiley moved over to the noticeboard and immediately saw the face of Black Bart staring out at him. John Smiley made a strange sound, something between a groan and a growl. 'That's the brute who killed my boy,' he said.

Beneath the ugly portrait he saw the words *Black Bart wanted Dead or Alive for murder. Reward 500 dollars*. John Smiley looked at the sheriff again. 'Let me tell you something, Sheriff. The brute who calls himself a man met us on the trail no more than three miles from here and that's where he struck the blow that killed my boy.'

'That's so, Mr Smiley,' Jack Kincade acknowledged.

'But what I can't figure is why he picked on us. We don't have much for any robber. We're just a bunch of travelling entertainers and we don't do harm to anybody.'

'That's true, Mr Smiley,' the sheriff agreed. 'I'm just sorry you had to meet that killer on the trail.'

But Jack Kincade was surprised as well. Why pick on an entertainer on the trail and gun whip his boy? It didn't make any kind of sense at all.

John Smiley shook his head. 'One thing's for sure, Mr Kincade, if those other *hombres* hadn't ridden up in time, we might have all been lying dead on the trail.'

'Which other *hombres*?' Doc Buchanan asked.

John Smiley pondered for a moment. 'A man called Adam Kirk.'

'Kirk!' Jack Kincade exclaimed.

John Smiley nodded. 'He and his buddy Charlie the Medic rode right back to town with us and then they branched off like they weren't too keen on riding in.'

Jack Kincade and Martin Buchanan exchanged glances.

'You know this man Kirk?' John Smiley asked them.

'We've met him once or twice,' Jack Kincade said with a tinge of irony.

John Smiley was thinking. 'The point being,' he said, 'I want to catch up on the man who killed my son.'

'You mean you want to track down on him?' Doc Buchanan asked him.

John Smiley knitted his eyebrows. 'I just want to bring him in so nobody else suffers like my boy.' He shook his head. 'I'm not interested in any reward. I just want justice, that's all.'

'Well, if you bring him in, you'll have to take the reward,' Jack Kincade said. 'It's part of the deal. But I should warn you, Mr Smiley, Black Bart is no castle of cards. If he sees you coming he'll shoot to kill. He's already shot three men to death and a fourth won't worry him one little bit. He'll just cut another notch in the butt of his gun.'

John Smiley raised his voice. 'I want to see that apology for a man swinging from the tallest tree on the range!' he said.

Jack Kincade laid a restraining hand on his arm. 'I understand how you feel, Mr Smiley, but you're an entertainer, not a gunman. Why don't you concentrate on what you're good at, and leave Black Bart to the law.'

John Smiley said, 'I appreciate your advice, Mr Kincade, and I'll think on it.'

29

*

In the back room behind the bar in the Long Branch Saloon Katie Smiley was talking to Sophia.

'My pa has never been so down since my ma died,' she said. 'I don't like to think what he might do.'

'Well, first off you have to take time to mourn,' Sophia said. 'And you must stay here just as long as you like.'

The funeral director had arrived promptly and removed John Smiley's body to the funeral parlour where it would rest until the funeral, which must be quite soon. Sudden death was not uncommon in Silver Spur, but since the murder of the Holtby family a year earlier things had been relatively quiet.

Katie Smiley was a brave young woman and she had been brought up not to show her feelings. Since her ma died she had held the family together as well as she could. She knew her father was a wonderful entertainer and a good man, but he needed support and she must provide it. And she wondered what he would do about the entertainment business, too.

In fact, Silver Spur provided an excellent funeral for the boy. Almost everyone in the township attended, and people came from far and wide to pay their respects. The little chapel was full to bursting point. John Smiley read a lesson and his voice was so steady some people said he was in denial.

Sophia had found Katie a black dress and bonnet to wear, but Katie took no part in the actual proceedings since people thought ladies were too delicate to attend funerals. With the assistance of Jack Kincade's wife Bridget, Sophia had conjured up a wonderful funeral supper that most folk tucked into with relish.

When Katie looked up she was surprised to see Adam Kirk standing close to her. He nodded and said nothing but his eyes spoke for him and he had a deeply expressive face.

'It's good of you to come, Mr Kirk,' Katie said.

Kirk smiled politely. 'Well, I had to come, didn't I? As soon as I heard I knew I must come. Charlie too. We both knew we must come as soon as we heard.'

Charlie the Medic approached, stetson in hand. 'I'm so sorry,' he said. 'I should have realized your brother needed more help than I could give.'

'You did your best,' she said. 'Nobody can do more than that.'

Charlie the Medic nodded. 'I know this isn't the place or time to say this, Miss Smiley, but you look as pretty as a picture. Isn't that so, Kirk?'

Kirk looked at Katie and smiled.

CHAPTER THREE

'What's happening about the show?' Tiny Broadhurst asked Kev Stanley after the funeral.

Kev Stanley looked at him in astonishment. Was there no end to this hulk's crass insensitivity? He pointed to the notice board.

'What does it say up there?' he asked Tiny.

Tiny shook his big head. 'Like I thought John Smiley would move on or cancel the show.'

'In which case you don't know John Smiley,' Kev told Tiny. 'You know what they say in show business: the show must go on.'

'Is that so?' Tiny marvelled. 'I ain't never heard that before.'

'There's a whole lot of things you never heard before,' Kev told him.

Tiny nodded. 'I understand it, though. I mean, in the war when we knew there was gonna be a battle we just had to pull us up by our boot straps, check our ammunition, and get on with the job. I guess that's what John Smiley has to do.'

'I guess so,' Kev said between clenched teeth.

On the morning after the funeral the whole of Silver

Spur seemed to be sleeping. Even the curs had gone to rest in the shade and there was scarcely a yap or a bark to be heard.

In fact things were far less straightforward than Kev Stanley had implied. Earlier he had broached the subject of the show with John Smiley. 'You need to rest up for a day or two,' he had said. 'Put the show on hold for a week at least.'

John Smiley had stared at him in horror. 'Give up the show?' he said in an uncharacteristically aggressive tone. 'Why the hell should I give up the show?'

'I just thought . . .' Kev saw a wild look in his friend's eye.

'I have to go on with the show!' John Smiley shouted. 'I have to go on with the show for my boy! Everybody must know that!'

Later, when Kev discussed it with his wife Sophia, she nodded wisely, 'People react in different ways to tragedy, Kev. Some men curl up and withdraw into themselves. Others get up and act. And John Smiley's the sort who gets up and acts.'

Kev couldn't argue with that, so he just kept his peace.

The show was scheduled for the next evening. Sophia and Katie sold tickets at the bar of the Long Branch Saloon. There were many murmurs of disapproval, and Tiny Broadhurst was heard to say that it was downright disrespectful to the dead boy. But everyone in the township bought a ticket, and when the evening came, the barn was so full some folk had to be turned away since there wasn't room even for a stray dog or cat.

Because the boy had died, it had to be a one man show. When John Smiley appeared from the wings – which were, in fact, a rather tattered black curtain Sophia had rigged up – there was an audible sigh from the audience. Was it sympathy or expectation? Nobody chose to say.

John Smiley strode to the centre of what passed for the stage. He took a deep bow and turned towards the old honky-tonk piano and waved his hand, and Katie Smiley struck a chord. Katie Smiley was not an accomplished pianist, but she knew how to strike out a tune and she played with unusual vigour as her father sang. His voice was rich and deep, and he sang loudly and defiantly as though he was throwing out a challenge to the whole universe.

Jack and Bridget Kincade were standing at the back of the barn with their two children, Stephanie and Gregory.

'You know what?' Jack Kincade said to his wife, 'That man has grit. He's singing like a whole cage full of lions.'

'He's singing like a man with a broken heart!' Bridget replied quietly.

Adam Kirk and Charlie the Medic were sitting close by. Charlie turned to Kirk and said, 'These people have true grit, Kirk. I've never heard anything like it! That girl can sure punish those ivories, and John Smiley sings like he's set to jump off the edge of the stage and fly to the sun.'

'You heard about the man who flew towards the sun and fell into the sea?' Kirk said.

'You mean the Greek guy?' Charlie replied.

'That's the one,' Kirk agreed. 'He had wings of wax and the wax melted.' But he wasn't looking at John Smiley: he was looking at Katie Smiley punishing the keys of the somewhat out-of-tune honky-tonk piano.

The performance came to an end and Katie and her father took a bow. The applause was rapturous, and some people roared and stamped their feet and threw up their hats. The cheering went on for more than a minute, but after the first bow, John Smiley disappeared behind the tattered black curtain and didn't reappear.

Katie stood by the piano and held up her hand as the applause died away. Then she spoke: 'Men and women,' she said, 'Good folk of Silver Spur . . . thank you . . . thank you so much.'

There was renewed applause. She held up her hand again and the crowd became quiet and expectant.

'Thank you,' she repeated. 'I thank you, not only for my father's sake but for my brother's sake. I know he'd be proud. So I thank you on his behalf too.' Then she waved to the audience and smiled.

'Well, I'll be damned!' Tiny Broadhurst said to nobody in particular – but nobody was listening, anyway. They were all jabbering like jackdaws under the barn roof.

Katie went out behind the black curtain and found her father sitting on a chair and gasping for breath. Doc Buchanan was standing over him ready to administer first aid. 'Take it easy,' the doc said. 'You've fought a great battle tonight and now you must rest. Take a deep breath and breathe out slowly.'

John Smiley wasn't listening: he was too busy fighting for breath. Then Sophia Stanley handed him a generous glass of rye whiskey and he drank it down in one gulp.

All over town folk were saying what a marvellous performance John Smiley and his daughter had given. It was indeed so memorable that some people hit the bottle too hard and needed to be carried home to bed. Among them was Tiny Broadhurst, who was rambling on about how he had won the Battle of Gettysburg almost single-handed when he passed out and fell off his stool. Carrying Tiny home would have been no mean feat, so they left him in the bar to sleep it off.

Next morning Jack Kincade was sitting in Bridget's Diner enjoying a hearty breakfast when a boy came over from the telegraph office. 'Excuse me, Sheriff,' the boy said, 'a message came through from River Fork. The boss says you should read it straightaway.' As he handed the paper over his expression was a mixture of apprehension and excitement.

Jack Kincade spread the paper and read the contents.

Hi Jack!
We had a robbery here yesterday afternoon. It was a bad business.
Three men held up the bank here and they shot dead the bank manager. Thought you should know in case the killers come down your way.
Your friend, Sheriff John Schnell

Jack Kincade looked at the boy. 'Tell the boss I'll be right over.'
Bridget was busy serving her customers. 'What happened?' she asked.
Jack told her the news. 'I'm going over to the telegraph office,' he said. He walked over to the telegraph office and sent a message to Sheriff Schnell.

Good morning, John!
Sorry to hear the bad news and thanks for the warning. Do you have a description of the killers? Was Black Bart the leader? And do you need help up there?
Please let me know. Jack.

As he walked over to Bridget's Diner again, he saw the familiar figure of John Smiley approaching from the direction of the Long Branch Saloon, and John Smiley was wearing a gunbelt with a shooter sitting half way down his leg.

'Good morning, John!' the sheriff said. 'I'm surprised to see you up and about so early. After that performance I thought you might be lying low and recovering your strength.'

John Smiley didn't smile. 'I don't think I'll ever sleep again,' he said. 'Not until this business is over and Black Bart is still and dead up on Boot Hill.'

Jack looked down at the shooter. 'I see you're packing artillery, sir. That's a little unusual for a man of peace, isn't it?'

'Well, you see, last night's performance might have been my last performance in this world.'

Jack Kincade shook his head. 'That's an awful big statement, John. I thought entertainers just faded away, and you've got an awful lot of entertaining to do before you hand over to the dark angel, so to speak.' He looked down at the gun. 'And if you're going to carry a gun, don't let it hang so low. It might look good, but if you meet Black Bart on a moonlit night, you need to have that shooter handy. So my advice would be to hitch it up a little higher, so you can reach down and bring it up in one sweeping movement.'

John Smiley grinned but he wasn't amused. 'I'll bear that in mind, Sheriff.'

Jack Kincade started back to Bridget's Diner. Then he turned. 'There's been a shooting up at River Fork.'

'Anyone killed?' John Smiley asked.

'They shot the bank manager up there. News just came through.'

'I know River Fork,' John Smiley said. 'We're booked in there for our next performance. So they killed Andy the bank manager?'

Jack Kincade paused. 'Sheriff Schnell sent a wire through. I don't know the details, just that the bank manager died of his wounds.'

John Smiley looked at the sky and reckoned it was going to be a fine day, but there were hints of cloud building in the west. 'How many men were in the bunch?' he asked.

'John Schnell said there were three.'

John Smiley smiled for the first time but it wasn't a happy smile. 'This is the voice of Providence, Jack,' he said. 'You don't need to tell me. The leader of that bunch was Black Bart.' He looked up at the sky again and shouted, 'Listen up, Black Bart, your dark angel is on its way.'

Katie Smiley was talking to Sophia Stanley in the room behind the bar. 'I'm really worried about my pa,' she said. 'I've never seen him like this before. Not even when my ma died. It's like he's been knocked right off his perch and has come up a different person. He's even wearing a gun. I knew he had one but I've never seen him wearing it before.'

'Give him time,' Sophia advised. 'A man like your father needs to go through a grieving process. We women grieve in a different way.'

Katie wasn't sure she understood that, but she didn't have much time to think about it because Kev Stanley appeared at the door. 'Excuse me, ladies, but there are two men asking to see you. Shall I show them through?'

The two women looked at one another and Sophia raised an eyebrow. Katie nodded. Then Adam Kirk and Charlie the Medic walked into the room.

'Good morning, ladies,' Adam Kirk said. Charlie the Medic gave a brief nod but said nothing.

Katie rose from her chair and curtsied, just like she did after a performance. 'Good morning, gentlemen.'

'What can we do for you?' Sophia asked.

Kirk stood with his broad-brimmed hat in his hand. Though he seemed at ease, Katie noticed that his fingers played nervously with the brim.

'We thought we'd just come by to pay our respects,' he said.

'That's right,' Charlie piped up. 'We were at the performance last night and we thought it was. . . .' He struggled to find the right word.

'Extraordinary,' Kirk prompted.

'And the way you spoke, Miss Smiley,' Charlie said. 'After what happened, that was truly remarkable!'

There was a momentary pause. 'Well, that's really kind of you, gentlemen,' Katie said. She was looking at Kirk and he was looking right back at her with a half smile on his lips.

'Well now,' Sophia said after a moment. 'Why don't you set yourselves down and take some refreshment.'

The two men exchanged glances and sat down.

Kirk looked at Katie and nodded as if to say, so far so good. 'Tell me, Miss Smiley, what are your plans for the future?' he asked.

Katie shrugged. 'That depends,' she said.

'I see.' Kirk nodded as though he understood.

Katie knew she had to say something, but she didn't know what. 'The truth is, Mr Kirk, I'm not sure what my pa has in mind. We're due in River Fork sometime, but my pa might not want to go on with the trip.'

'Understandably, Miss Smiley,' he said. 'Things are tough for you at the moment.'

Then Sophia reappeared with a pot of coffee and two cups and saucers on a tray. She put them on the table and turned to Charlie. 'Kev would like a word with you, Mr. . . .' she said.

'The name's Franklin,' he reminded her. 'Charlie Franklin.'

Sophia made a sideways motion with her head and Charlie took the hint. 'I'll just walk through and talk to Kev,' he said. Though he didn't exactly wink, Katie saw his eyelid droop a little.

'Why don't we drink our coffee, Miss Smiley?' Kirk asked with a smile. 'After all, I see Mrs Stanley brought out the best cups and saucers for our benefit.'

Katie poured out the coffee and handed him a cup and saucer. Was his hand shaking slightly as he accepted it?

'Is your pa around?' he asked.

'Pa just went out for a moment,' she said. Then she added almost without thinking. 'I'm worried about him, Mr Kirk. He was wearing a gun. I've never seen that before.' Her voice faltered as she spoke.

Kirk looked at her and smiled, and his smile almost melted her heart; it was full of understanding and concern. For a moment neither of them spoke. Then Kirk said, 'You're a brave young woman, Miss Smiley.' He was about to add something, but she held up her hand stop him.

'Thanks for coming, Mr Kirk. I really appreciate it. Why

don't you have another cup of Sophia's excellent coffee?'

He smiled. 'I do believe I will, Miss Smiley. I do believe I will.'

Jack Kincade was back in Bridget's Diner drinking a coffee and chewing on one of Bridget's rock cakes. They were hard on the outside and soft and sweet on the inside, just like Bridget herself, and Jack really enjoyed them.

'What's on you mind?' Bridget asked him.

'Nothing in particular,' he said.

Bridget gave a sceptical grin. 'When you say "nothing in particular" I know you have something very particular on your mind. And, by the way, that's your third rock cake this morning. You're getting a little too heavy round the middle, d'you know that?'

Jack Kincade swallowed the last of his rock cake. 'You're right, of course,' he reflected. 'I *am* worried about two things, apart from my waistline. First, I'm worried about my friend John Schnell up at River Fork after the bank robbery and the shooting of the bank manager. Remember what happened a year back after the Holtby massacre. John got himself shot. Luckily he survived, but he's never been the same man since.'

Bridget nodded sagely. 'I understand that,' she said. 'What's the other worry?'

'The other worry is John Smiley. I think the man's gone slightly off his head.'

'Why d'you say that?'

Jack gave a grim smile. 'I met him this morning and he was toting a gun. That's completely out of character with John Smiley. I don't know if he can shoot straight, but if he meets Black Bart on a dark night he will certainly need to. From what I know about Black Bart he wouldn't think

41

twice about shooting a man in the head or the back. That's the sort of man he is.'

'Well, Jack,' his wife said, 'You don't need to worry about that unless he shows up here. After the Holtby massacre you promised me you were going to give up the sheriff's badge and retire. But you're still here, strutting your stuff.'

Jack waggled his head from side to side and grinned. 'Well, I can't picture myself sitting in an armchair, smoking a pipe and getting fatter like Tiny Broadhurst. I don't think that's quite my style.'

Bridget punched him lightly on the shoulder and laughed.

'So you're going up to River Fork?' Kev Stanley said to John Smiley.

John Smiley shrugged his shoulders. 'Life must go on, Mr Stanley, and we must roll along with it, mustn't we?'

Kev Stanley agreed. He thought he would go on running the Long Branch Saloon until he fell right off the bar and died. That's the way life was, wasn't it?

'See you're still wearing that shooter,' Kev observed.

John Smiley grimaced. 'You don't know who you might meet on the trail, do you?' he replied.

'That is so,' Kev agreed.

When all the polite 'good byes' and 'ride safe' had been said, John Smiley and Katie got up on the driving seat of the wagon, ready to drive on, when Adam Kirk and Charlie the Medic appeared on their horses.

'Good morning,' Kirk said. 'We hear you're going to drive up to River Fork.'

'That is so,' John Smiley said. 'We have a show to do up there.'

'Well, that's just fine,' Charlie said. 'As it happens we're on our way there, too. So maybe you wouldn't mind if we ride along with you.'

'Not at all,' John Smiley said. 'Indeed, you're welcome, sirs.'

Katie glanced at Kirk and tried to suppress a blush, but it wasn't easy.

It was early next morning and John Schnell, Sheriff of River Fork, was sitting in his office doing his accounts when his wife looked in. 'John, I've just seen those entertainers riding in on their wagon.'

John got up from his desk and looked through the window on to Main Street. He had received a wire from his friend Jack Kincade, so he was expecting John Smiley. He knew John Smiley well and had seen his performances before. Jack Kincade had told him about the death of Smiley's son, John Smiley Junior. So when he and his wife stepped out on to the sidewalk, he was a little surprised to see the entertainer wearing a gunbelt and his daughter Katie toting a Winchester rifle beside him on the wagon seat. He was also surprised to see Adam Kirk and Charlie the Medic riding with them.

'Goot morning!' he shouted to John Smiley. 'Goot morning, Miss Katie!' He still spoke with quite a strong German accent, though he had been in America since he was only twenty years old.

John Smiley climbed down from the rig and gripped Schnell's hand. 'Good morning, my friend.'

John Schnell looked down at John Smiley's gunbelt. 'I don't think I ever saw you carrying a gun before, my friend.'

John Smiley nodded. 'I don't think I've ever worn one

before, Sheriff.' He was clearly in no mood for pleas-
antries.

Katie had climbed down from the wagon with the assistance of Adam Kirk. She and the sheriff's wife embraced.
'Come right in,' Mrs Schnell said.

'Thank you,' Katie said. The sheriff's wife thought she
looked somewhat pale, which wasn't surprising in view of
the circumstances.

John Smiley and Katie walked through the sheriff's
office to the back room, where Mrs Schnell served refreshments.

Kirk and Charlie the Medic stood outside talking to
Sheriff Schnell.

'So they robbed the bank,' Kirk said.

'Yeah, the whole town's in mourning,' Sheriff Schnell
told him.

'You sure it was Black Bart?' Kirk asked.

'Not much doubt about that,' Sheriff Schnell said. 'I
didn't see them myself, but the description fits. They just
shot the manager down when he refused to hand over the
key to the safe. Andy the manager was a brave man, but he
lost his life in vain because the teller handed over the key
just the same. They got away with quite a haul.' He
nodded sagaciously. 'Andy was the most popular man in
town. So we're all in a state of shock.'

Charlie the Medic spoke up. 'Well, if they got away with
a heap of dollars, one thing's for sure: they're not going to
open a savings account – they'll just spend like it's the end
of the world.'

'That is so,' Sheriff Schnell said. 'Well now, why don't
you just step inside and take a glass of my wife's fine home
brew?'

Kirk and Charlie the Medic were only too keen to oblige.

*

The township of River Fork was quite a lot bigger than Silver Spur, and it boasted a hall that was used to stage events and to hold a trial when necessary. And that was where John Smiley was to give his next performance. It even had a piano, which, though not grand, was perhaps a little more tuneful than Kev Stanley's piano in Silver Spur.

Katie Smiley was in the hall practising next morning when she turned round and saw Kirk standing in the doorway, smiling somewhat uncertainly. She stopped playing immediately and met his eye.

'Please don't stop playing, Miss Smiley. I like to hear it,' he said.

Katie felt her face starting to glow. 'I don't like people to listen when I'm practising, Mr Kirk.'

'Well then, I won't listen. Maybe we could talk a little.' He raised an enquiring eyebrow.

Katie stood up and found she was shaking slightly. 'I guess we could,' she said quietly. What was he going to say? she wondered. She noticed Charlie the Medic wasn't with him: why was that? she wondered.

Kirk opened his mouth and was about to speak, but what he wanted to say never got said because at that moment they heard a shot.

Kirk strode to the door and threw it open, and Katie followed. Her father John was staggering and firing his revolver, but there was no target: he was just firing it in the air. Sheriff Schnell was standing some distance behind him. His gun was drawn but he just held it down against his side.

John Smiley raised his gun somewhat unsteadily and fired another shot, this time straight down Main Street.

Fortunately nobody was in the line of fire, so nobody got hit.

'Oh, my God!' Katie cried, 'What's he doing?'

Kirk stepped out on to Main Street and walked towards John Smiley.

'Don't go near!' Katie cried. 'You'll get yourself killed!'

She needn't have worried, because at that moment John Smiley pitched forwards and fell on his face.

Kirk walked towards him and picked up the gun.

'Drunk!' Sheriff Schnell said.

Kirk inspected the gun and stuck it under his belt. 'What are you going to do?'

'Well, what we do is hoist him up on his feet and put him in the town calaboose to sober up.'

Between them they dragged John Smiley to his feet. He looked at his daughter through bleary eyes and tried to speak. 'What happened. . . ?' he slurred, and then he passed out.

'Please don't put him in jail, Sheriff!' Katie pleaded. 'Put him in the wagon and I'll take care of him.'

Sheriff John Schnell hesitated and then looked at Kirk, and Kirk nodded and said, 'We'll take good care of him, Sheriff.'

CHAPTER FOUR

Some miles upriver from River Fork, Black Bart and his two henchmen, Steve and Mart, had pitched camp and were having a fry-up in a soot-blackened pan. Black Bart never did any cooking himself; he left that to Mart. He had laid a blanket on the ground and was counting out the dollars from the hold-up in River Fork.

'Looks like we did pretty well,' Steve said.

'Pity you had to shoot the bank manager,' Mart said from behind the cooking pot.

'I didn't shoot the guy,' Black Bart growled.

'Well, he sure didn't shoot himself,' Steve joked.

Black Bart gave Steve a warning glance. 'It don't matter who pulled the trigger,' he said, 'If I pulled the trigger I pulled it for the three of us – and he deserved it, anyway, the manager!' His face had gone purple behind the black beard that suited his character so well.

Steve saw a red light flashing in his head so he backed off. He knew what Black Bart was like when he went into a rage.

'What are you complaining about, anyways?' Black Bart asked him.

Steve gave him a reassuring smile, 'I ain't complaining,

Bart, I'm just saying.'

'Well, don't say it again!' Black Bart roared.

'OK, Bart,' Mart said from behind the soot-blackened pan. 'Let's cool it, shall we? Chuck's nearly ready to dish out.' In fact, quite an appetizing aroma was beginning to drift across the camp. Food always put Bart into a better mood and he almost smiled.

'OK, then, dish it out, for Gawd's sake.' His two *compadres* exchanged glances and grinned; they knew Black Bart better than he knew himself.

Steve was the leaner of the two; he had been a waddy on a ranch down Texas way. He knew about horses and steers, but his roving spirit had driven him into crime from which he hoped to get rich and retire, probably to California where he'd heard the climate was good.

By contrast, Mart was the son of a small-time store-keeper who never had a dime to his name. So Mart had lit out for the hills in search of a better deal, and had met Black Bart in a saloon. In those days Bart had looked quite a smart dude, but you would never think of crossing him in case he brought his huge fist down on your head and knocked you right into the next county. Mart had been amazed when the entertainer John Smiley had actually out-boxed Black Bart and knocked him to the ground. It was like seeing a magic mountain crumbling to dust! Mart would have shot the entertainer, but he was secretly glad he had survived.

'OK, Bart, what happens next?' he asked Black Bart.

'What d'you mean, *what happens next?*' Black Bart said in a none-too-pleasant manner.

'Well, what I mean is, what happens after we've divvied out the greenbacks?'

Bart gave him a suspicious glance. 'You two get your

share, and I get a cut off the top since I'm the brains of the outfit.'

'Do we get enough to retire?' Steve chipped in.

Black Bart grinned broadly and showed his rotting teeth, which gave him a deal of trouble from time to time.

'Depends how you want to live,' he said. 'If you don't mind living like a pig in a pile of shit, then maybe you've got enough. But if you're a tad more ambitious and want to retire to California or some place and live it up on cigars and whiskey in the sun, then you're in for a big disappointment, my son.'

'So, you mean we should do another bank?' Steve the ex-wrangler asked.

Black Bart pondered for a moment. 'I've been thinking on that,' he said.

Mart and Steve exchanged glances.

'What conclusions have you come to?' Mart asked him.

A crafty smile spread over the big man's visage. 'My conclusion is we ride down to Silver Spur and hit the bank there.'

Mart and Steve looked at one another again.

'Why Silver Spur?' Mart asked Bart.

A strange gleam came into Bart's eye.

'What are you thinking?' Steve asked him.

'What I'm thinking is, if I'm gonna retire and live the good life, I need a few home comforts around me, which means I shall need a good woman . . . by my side, so to speak.'

Mart and Steve looked at one another in some surprise. 'You mean like marriage?' Mart asked.

Black Bart showed his rotten teeth again. 'Not necessarily,' he said. 'Just a woman to warm my bed and everything else a woman can do.' At that point he almost

49

winked, which wasn't a pretty sight.

'That sounds like a crazy idea to me,' Steve said.

'What's wrong with the calico queens?' Mart asked.

'There ain't nothing wrong with those queens,' Bart said, 'as far as they go. But they ain't gonna warm your slippers by the fire, are they?'

There was a moment of rather horrified silence.

'Well now,' Mart said, 'do you have anyone particular in mind?'

Bart was still showing his rotting teeth. 'Matter of fact I do,' he said.

'Anyone we know?' Mart asked.

Bart nodded. 'Remember that young woman we met on the trail, John Smiley's girl?'

The two men looked at one another in dismay.

'You can't be serious, Bart!' Mart said.

'Oh, I'm serious,' the big man replied. 'And for two reasons. First is, I liked that girl's style. She had a lot of grit, and that's what I want in a woman.'

'And what's the other reason?' Steve asked.

'The other reason is, I have in mind to get back on that guy John Smiley for what happened on the trail just outside Silver Spur.'

'How are you gonna do that?' Mart asked him.

'Well, I have a plan in mind,' Black Bart replied with a toothy grin.

But before Black Bart could elaborate on his plan, Steve said, 'Look out there!'

Their eyes turned towards the river where they saw two men in a birch-bark canoe. They wore beaver hats like backwoodsmen, and they were just paddling along minding their own business, probably on a fishing trip. The river wasn't too wide at this point, and it looped away to the right just where Black Bart and his two sidekicks were camped.

One of the two canoemen glanced in their direction and muttered something to his companion. Then he shouted, 'Mind if we come ashore?'

Mart and Steve looked at Bart for guidance. 'I wouldn't recommend it,' Bart shouted back in a gravely tone.

'Only this is the best place for fishing,' the man said.

'We don't do a lot of fishing,' Bart growled. 'We just set here awhile minding our business and cooking up whatever's in the pot.'

The two men turned the canoe and paddled towards the shore. They leaped out of the canoe and beached it on the gravel no more than a hundred feet away.

'Well,' one of them said, 'We won't disturb you, gentlemen. We'll just do a little fishing and then move along out.'

Bart nodded and said nothing, though he didn't look any too pleased.

Mart said quietly to Steve, 'It's a little late in the day for fishing, ain't it?'

Steve said. 'Maybe they aim to set up camp.'

Bart had been listening. 'Where are you boys from?' he shouted.

The two men seemed to be busy with their fishing gear. 'Downriver,' one of them shouted back.

'Whereabouts downriver?' Bart shouted back. 'Wouldn't be River Fork, would it?'

The two men conferred quietly. Then the younger man, who did most of the talking said, 'No, not River Fork – someplace else further along.'

Mart, who was looking intently at the fishermen, muttered quietly to Bart, 'That "someplace further along" is a damned lie.'

Bart nodded in agreement. 'I guess you're damn right,' he growled. They looked at the two men and saw they were loading their fishing gear into the canoe again. The younger man looked in their direction. 'Change of plan,' he shouted. 'It's time we went home to roost.'

The two men launched the canoe and started paddling hell for leather. They seemed in a hurry to get away.

'You know what I think,' Mart said.

'What do you think, knucklehead?'

'I think those *hombres* don't know a fish from a bear,' Mart said.

'Another thing,' Steve added. 'I have a shrewd suspicion they know who we are.'

Bart narrowed his eyes, which was always a bad sign. 'You could be right on that,' he said.

'So what do we do now?' Mart asked him.

'We have to make sure and shoot them,' Bart said.

He reached for his Winchester carbine.

'They weren't bothering us none,' Steve protested.

Bart was checking his Winchester. 'Didn't you learn nothing on that ranch in Texas?' he said.

'Well, I learned to be wary with steers,' Steve said.

Bart gave a gritty laugh. Then he raised his Winchester and trained it on the rapidly retreating men in the canoe. As Bart took aim, the younger man looked towards Bart and shouted something to his companion. They had started to paddle more furiously when Bart fired a shot. 'Damn it! I missed,' he shouted. He levered the carbine and fired another shot. This time it hit the canoe.

The two men leaped out of the canoe and made for the opposite shore.

'Shoot the bastards!' Bart roared. And he fired another shot.

Fortunately for the two fishermen they were quite close to the shore, so they kept wading and soon hoisted themselves up on to the bank. The canoe was holed below the waterline and was sinking.

'What are you waiting for!' Bart roared to Steve and Mart. 'Grab your guns and shoot the bastards!'

Mart and Steve reached for their weapons, but it was too late: the two fishermen were already disappearing among the trees.

'What's wrong with you two knuckleheads!' Bart roared. He ran down to the creek just as fast as his fat legs would carry him, levelled his Winchester and popped off two quick shots – but it was too late: the two fishermen were half visible between the branches. 'Goddamn!' he shouted, and pumped off a couple more shots at the sinking canoe.

Bart then sat down beside the fire and checked his ammunition. 'If you two knuckleheads had got your act together those two *hombres* would have been belly up in the water by now.'

'Well,' Mart said, 'I guess they can't get far. It's a long walk back to River Fork, specially after sundown and through the trees. They'll most likely meet a grizzly on the way.'

All three of them almost died from laughter at the thought of those two fishermen being chased by a bear all the way back to River Fork.

In fact the two fishermen had a lot more 'bush savvy' than Black Bart and his sidekicks had imagined. They were now sitting by the river not too far off. The young man who had done most of the talking was drying his clothes over a fire the older man had built. The younger man was Hank Holden, and the older man was Jesse

Jessimore, his father-in-law, and they both came from River Fork.

'Well, Pa,' Hank said, 'I guess we're lucky we've still got our skins on our bodies.'

'Well,' the older man said. 'Those guys were intent on puncturing those skins you just mentioned. Alice and Grace would have been grieved out of the minds if we hadn't made it back.'

Hank shook his head. 'Well, we haven't made it back yet, and it's a long ways. So we'd better start walking pretty quick, unless we want to spend the night in these here woods.' He looked across at his father-in-law. 'Lucky you managed to get the fire going. The trouble is, we don't have any food supplies.'

Jesse Jessimore nodded. 'That's a problem,' he agreed, 'but as you said, we have our skins, and having your skin has a lot to recommend it.'

'That's true,' Hank said. 'You know who those *hombres* were, Pa?'

'I have a strong suspicion,' Jesse said. 'I do believe those three scaramouches were the men who robbed the bank in River Fork last week and killed my friend Andy, the manager.'

'And there's quite a big reward on that big guy's head, dead or alive for murder, it says on the poster.'

'Pity we don't have shooters,' Jesse said. 'Then we could double back and take a pop at him.'

'I don't think that's the best idea,' Hank said. 'Lucky for us they can't shoot straight. Otherwise we'd be lying back there waiting for the coyotes to strip the flesh from our bones.'

Jesse shuddered. 'Did anyone ever tell you you have a morbid sense of humour?' he asked his son-in-law.

*

It was well after sunrise next morning when Alice and Grace showed up at the sheriff's office. Alice was Hank Holden's wife and Grace was her mother.

'What can I do for you, ladies?' Sheriff Schnell asked them.

'We're worried about our menfolk,' Alice explained. Then she told him the two men had left during the previous afternoon and paddled downriver on a fishing trip, but they hadn't returned.

Sheriff Schnell always tried to look on the bright side. 'Maybe they decided to camp out for the night,' he suggested.

Grace shook her head. 'I don't think so, Sheriff. I have a strong feeling they've met with some kind of accident. I've always said that canoe was far too frail, but they wouldn't listen to me.'

John Schnell knew about birch-bark canoes and wilderness trips. He'd once boasted he'd caught the biggest fish in the lake! 'I guess those boys will come back safe and sound,' he said.

The two women walked back to their cabins convinced that the sheriff was a useless chunk of mankind wearing a badge of office he wasn't capable of living up to.

John Smiley woke that morning with a very sore head, and when he tried to get out of bed his head spun like a top and he threw up. Luckily his daughter Katie was there to steady him.

'What happened?' he asked her.

'You got drunk as a skunk,' she said, 'and you tried to shoot up the town. But luckily you were too drunk to hit anyone. The sheriff was going to throw you in gaol but we managed to persuade him to let you lie here.'

'Who's "we"?' he asked feebly.

'Mr Kirk was a great help. He walked right out on Main Street before you could shoot anyone and took the gun from you.'

As they were speaking there was a knock on the wagon door and Adam Kirk and Charlie the Medic appeared.

'You feeling better, Mr Smiley?' Kirk asked with a grin.

'You want to know the truth, I'm feeling like I swallowed shit,' John Smiley admitted.

'Take another drink,' Charlie the Medic advised. 'Some say it helps but I'm not sure about that.'

John Smiley shivered. 'Thank you. I don't think so.' His head was beginning to spin again. 'What's happening to me?' he asked.

'You're suffering from grief, sir,' Kirk said. 'It hits folk in different ways.'

'I guess you're right,' John Smiley said with a groan.

Some time around midday two men walked into town. They were Hank Holden and his father-in-law Jesse Jessimore. Both were in reasonable shape and both were tuckered out and ravenously hungry.

'What in heaven's name happened to you?' Grace asked her husband in dismay.

As usual Hank did most of the talking, and he told Alice and Grace what had happened. Alice threw her arms around her husband and hugged him. 'Thank heavens you're safe!' she cried.

Grace wasn't so kind. She had become used to her husband's escapades and she wasn't particularly tolerant. 'So they shot the canoe from under you?' she said.

'They were trying to shoot us!' Jesse protested. 'That big guy fired straight at us. My guess is he knew we'd recognized him. It was the bunch that held up the bank the other day and shot Andy.'

'Well, that sure is something!' Grace admitted. 'Alice, why don't you walk over and talk to the sheriff while I feed up these two men?'

Alice didn't need asking twice. She walked right over to the sheriff's office and almost collided with Kirk and Charlie the Medic on the way.

Charlie raised his hat. 'Good day to you, madame.'

'Good day to you, sir!' Alice didn't bother to curtsey, but rushed into the sheriff's office.

'So the boys got back safely,' he said with his hands hooked into his braces.

'It's them!' she cried.

John Schnell looked puzzled. 'Well, I saw them, Mrs Holden.'

'No, sheriff,' she cried. 'I'm talking about the bank robbers, that man they call Black Bart. He took a shot at them and nearly killed them.' Then she burst into tears.

John Schnell frowned. 'I see,' he said. 'I think I'd better step across Main Street and get the full picture.'

Adam Kirk and Charlie the Medic were sitting in the shade under the ramada drinking cool drinks when they saw Sheriff Schnell approaching.

'Did somebody steal your apricots?' Charlie the Medic asked him.

John Schnell didn't go great guns on humour in a crisis. 'I think we might have a fix on those bank robbers,' he said. 'I'm just going across the street to see the two men who say they've seen Black Bart and his two sidekicks.'

Kirk got to his feet in time to see Alice Holden scurrying towards him. 'That Black Bart!' she cried. 'He took a shot at my husband when he was fishing.'

Charlie the Medic and Kirk looked at one another and nodded. Then they both followed the sheriff.

Hank Holden and Jesse Jessimore were eating their meal when the sheriff and Charlie the Medic and Kirk appeared.

'This good lady tells me Black Bart and his two sidekicks gunned down on you yesterday. Would you care to fill me in on the details?' the sheriff asked.

As usual Hank did most of the talking. He told the sheriff what had happened with considerable elaboration. According to him Black Bart had been so close to them that they had to dive into the middle of the river and swim to save their skins. Jesse Jessimore didn't bother to contradict him. He was too busy wiping his plate round with a hunk of his wife's home-baked bread.

'Where was this exactly?' the sheriff asked.

Then Jesse Jessimore spoke up. 'Some ten miles downstream from here. A sort of bend where it's good for fishing. Our canoe had most of our gear on board so it might still be close to the side of the river.'

John Schnell was a keen fisherman himself. 'I think I know the place,' he said. 'Been fishing up there myself a few times.' He looked at Kirk. 'Maybe we should ride it there and mosey around a little. What you think, Kirk?'

Kirk shrugged. 'My guess is Black Bart will be long gone from there. He won't stick around after what happened.'

'He might be stupid, but he's not completely off his chump,' Charlie the Medic added.

Katie Smiley was sitting with her father in the wagon. 'This has got to stop,' she said to him.

John Smiley looked at her and sighed. 'You sound just like your ma,' he said.

'A pity she didn't lay down the law a little more firmly,' she replied sharply.

John Smiley didn't want to contradict her. 'So,' he said, 'what do you expect me to do?'

She shook her head. 'First you've got to give up the bottle. Boozing up like you've been doing won't bring back my brother. You've got to learn to accept that he's gone and he's not coming back.'

Her father gave a rueful shake of his head. 'I guess you're right.' She saw he was close to tears.

'The other thing is you've got to stop shooting up the place, and put that gun somewhere safe. You could have killed somebody yesterday, and you know what happens to gunmen. Those who take up the gun will die by the gun.'

John Smiley shook his head. 'If only I knew where that apology for a man was . . .'

'Pa, stop thinking about him,' she said sternly, 'otherwise you'll be good for nothing. What about the show? It would grieve Johnny if you gave up the show, and at the moment you're in no fit state to do a show.'

John Smiley looked alarmed and then thoughtful. 'I can do the show!' he insisted. 'By tomorrow night I'll be ready, just as I was in Silver Spur.'

'I hope so,' she said, 'Just as long as you stop drinking and shooting the place up. You're an entertainer, not a gunman.'

Black Bart and his two sidekicks were some distance north but not too far from the river. They were riding close to a thick stand of cottonwoods when Steve held up his hand

and they stopped.

'What gives?' Black Bart demanded but there was no time for an answer. Four riders emerged from the trees ahead of them, and they were all well tooled up. The leader held up his arm in greeting. He was wearing an old pair of wire-rimmed spectacles and he had mutton-chop whiskers that stopped just above the corners of his mouth. He looked like a man who fancied himself as some kind of dandy.

'Why, my dear God above!' he declared in a well articulated voice as though he were practising to be an English lord, 'If it ain't my old buddy Bartholomew Baldrig.'

Black Bart grinned. He hated the name Bartholemew, thought it sounded kind of girlish. As for Baldrig, he wasn't too keen on that either, since he had a thick mop of black hair and a fearsome black beard. 'So we meet again, Alphonso Sebastian,' he replied with a sarcastic grin.

Alphonso Sebastian gave a chirping sort of laugh. 'Heard you were in these parts,' he crowed, 'but didn't reckon to catch up with you so soon.'

'That's my pleasure,' Bart chortled back.

Alphonso nodded. 'I heard about your doings, Bartholomew. You're getting quite a reputation in these parts.'

'Maybe I am,' Bart acknowledged without undue modesty. He was thinking about the price on his head, which no doubt Alphonso was well aware of. Around ten years earlier he and Alphonso had ridden together, and Bart knew Alphonso was a somewhat slippery character who would sell his mother down the river for little more than two hundred dollars.

'Do you have plans for the future?' Alphonso enquired, and he gave a kind of half wink which was characteristic.

'Nothing to mention,' Bart said. He gave his sidekicks a glance to see whether they were ready for any trouble. Mart already had his hand on his holster, ready to draw if necessary. He, too, knew of Alphonso's reputation as a devious and dangerous character.

'Now then,' Alphonso said, 'how are you boys doing for supplies?'

'Enough to keep our bellies from flapping against our backbones,' Bart replied. 'What's it to you, anyways?'

Alphonso grinned like a high-class chimp wearing glasses. 'Thought you might like to join us in a little chow. How would that be?'

Bart looked at Mart, and Mart raised an eyebrow. 'You got meat?' he asked.

Alphonso gave a chirpy kind of laugh. 'We've got everything,' he said. 'You give it a name, we've got it. Ain't that the case, boys?'

'We've got it,' one of his gang echoed. And the others laughed none too pleasantly.

'What's on your mind?' Mart asked him.

Alphonso squinted at him. 'I don't recall meeting you before, my man,' he said in a lordly fashion.

'And I don't recall meeting you, either,' Mart retorted. 'But I know who you are.'

Alphonso switched to Bart again. 'You meet all kinds on the trail, don't you, my son. Things aren't exactly what they used to be in the old times, are they?'

Black Bart gave him a hard scowl. 'Listen up, Mister Sebastian,' he growled. 'Why don't we cut the crap and get down to business. Why don't you come clean on what you really want.'

Alphonso chortled. 'That's what I always liked about you, Bartholomew. Straight down the middle, no messing.

You speak your mind. So let me do the same. Truth is, we've been tracking down on you ever since you did that bank job in River Fork. Thought we might throw in with you and become a team. After all, four and three adds up to seven if my counting is right.'

Bart raised his ugly brow. 'So you're suggesting we work as a team.'

Alphonso chortled again. 'Your brain is working a whole lot better than it was when we last rode together, Bartholomew.'

Black Bart was still scowling. 'Do we join you, or do you join us?' he demanded.

'You mean who's gonna be boss man.' He shrugged. 'That doesn't matter a bean to me.'

Black Bart grinned. 'Well, that's OK as long as you stop calling me Bartholomew.'

'OK, Bart, that's a deal.'

Alphonso reached over and they shook hands.

CHAPTER FIVE

John Smiley was sitting in the saloon, but he wasn't drinking; he was thinking about the evening's performance. Kirk was sitting across from him, but he wasn't drinking either; he was chewing on a cigar Kev Stanley had given him, though he never smoked.

'I wanted to ask you something,' Kirk said to John Smiley.

'Ask away,' John Smiley replied. He was going over his lines in his head, something he had rarely done before; normally the show just went on and he improvised his way through it. But to tell the truth, the last several days had made a deep impression on him, and for the first time his confidence had drained away, like water out of a bath.

'It's about your daughter Katherine,' Kirk said.

John Smiley never called Katie Katherine, so he was a little surprised. He looked at Kirk and smiled and nodded. 'We call her Katie, always have done.'

Kirk bit hard on his cigar and nodded. 'Well, OK, Mr Smiley. Katie sounds a whole lot better.'

'Plays the piano like an angel,' John Smiley reflected. 'Don't know what I'd do without her, you know that?'

'She sure can play,' Kirk agreed. 'How did she learn that?'

'It's a natural gift, Mr Kirk. Just like it came down to her from the heavenly spheres, if you can believe that.'

Kirk nodded. He hadn't thought much about the heavenly spheres but he'd thought a whole lot about Katie Smiley. In fact he couldn't get her out of his mind. 'Well,' he said, 'that's what I wanted to talk to you about.'

John Smiley was smiling reflectively. 'Takes after her mother, you know.'

'She must have been an admirable lady, Mr Smiley.'

'She could play the piano real well. Pity we couldn't afford to buy an instrument. Now she's gone I realize she had a tough deal with me on the road. She was a real good woman and I didn't deserve her, you know.'

'I'm sure you did your best, Mr Smiley.' Kirk took a breath and was about to speak again.

'Keeps me in line, you know, Mr Kirk,' John Smiley interrupted.

Kirk smiled and shook his head. 'That's exactly what I wanted to speak to you about, Mr Smiley.'

There was a pause that seemed to Kirk to last for ever. John Smiley regarded him carefully as if for the first time. 'Well, it's up to you, my boy.'

'I don't know what you mean,' Kirk said.

'Well, what I'm trying to say is, it's not up to me, it's up to you.'

A coin seemed to slot right into Kirk's head. 'You mean you have no objection, Mr Smiley?'

John Smiley grinned. 'Oh, I have a whole bunch of objections, Mr Kirk, but if you want to marry my daughter it's up to you to ask her. After all, she's the one who'll have to put up with you, isn't she?'

Kirk nodded. 'Thank you, Mr Smiley,' he said.

*

That night the barn was full even to overflowing. Everyone in town wanted to see what this gun-toting entertainer could do, apart from getting drunk and firing off his gun, fortunately without hitting anyone. Many people had seen his earlier performances, and wondered why John Smiley had changed so much. Some had heard about the tragedy of John Smiley Junior's death, and these wondered how John Smiley could walk on to what passed for a stage and tell jokes and sing comic songs with nods and winks at the audience. 'Hasn't the guy got no feelings?' one man was heard to say. 'The show has got to go on,' replied another, who prided himself on his knowledge of the theatre.

The truth was that John Smiley was more at home on the stage than anywhere else, and as soon as he trod the boards he became a different man. It was in his blood, so to speak.

Katie was partly stung by the Thespian bug, too. The old upright piano in River Fork was so tottery and out of tune that only a musical saint could have coaxed a melody out of it. But Katie somehow managed to produce a sort of honky-tonk tune that the people of River Fork loved. After each selection they roared with approval, and some threw their hats in the air while others hurled coins and dollar bills on to the stage, which John Smiley gathered up in his hat.

Kirk was sitting at the back of the hall with Sheriff Schnell and his family and Charlie the Medic.

'That young gel plays like an angel with silver fingers,' the sheriff said.

Kirk didn't reply. He was too busy falling in love with

Katie and thinking about the somewhat inconclusive conversation he had had with John Smiley. And he was also looking round at the audience, some of whom were strikingly bizarre characters.

'You seen all these folks before?' he asked John Schnell.

'Well, most of them are townsfolk, but some have ridden in from different parts. River Fork is a growing town and you never know who you're going to meet. It's that sort of place, you know, Mr Kirk.'

In fact there was one face in particular that attracted Kirk's attention. It was one of Alphonso's sidekicks called Gus Merriweather, a tall, rangy character with wide mutton-chop whiskers of which he was inordinately proud. In fact he reminded Kirk of a peacock, the way he strutted about looking down on everyone as though he owned the whole of River Fork.

'Did you ever see that *hombre* before?' Kirk asked Sheriff Schnell.

'Can't say I have,' John Schnell replied. 'Looks like a banker or a lawyer to me. Maybe he's looking over the place to set up business in town.'

In fact Gus Merriweather had indeed studied the law, but when he failed an exam he had abandoned the law and fallen in with Alphonso. After all, if a man could strike the jackpot by bending the law, why bother to play it straight?

Kirk turned to Charlie the Medic. 'Have you seen that strutting turkey before?' he asked.

'I think I might have seen him,' Charlie said. 'Looks kind of professional, like a banker or something, except for the gun at his side.'

Kirk saw the shooter strapped to the man's side in a well worn holster. 'You've got a point there, Charlie,' he said.

Honest bankers don't carry guns, so Kirk got to thinking about the *hombre* with the mutton-chop whiskers. Had he seen him before? Had it been on a wanted poster somewhere? Nothing came to mind, but Kirk was by no means reassured. He had a nose for criminals and criminality. 'I have a hunch about that guy,' he said to Charlie the Medic.

Charlie the Medic twitched his nose like a wolf sensing danger. 'You think he's come into town to find out what's doing?' he asked Kirk.

'I don't know about that,' Kirk said. 'But I do know one thing, and that's that Black Bart and his men were seen on the river just two days back and they weren't fishing. I have a suspicion this fancy guy might be connected with them in some way.'

'What makes you think that?' Charlie asked him.

Kirk shook his head. 'It's just a feeling I have. Why don't you buy the guy a drink and see what you can pick up?'

Charlie raised his eyebrows and waggled his head. He had been with Kirk a long time and sometimes Kirk's suspicions worked out well, which was why a number of bad men were behind bars or under the earth on Boot Hill. So he made his way over to the bar during the interval until he was standing right next to the man with the mutton-chop whiskers. Merriweather turned to glance at him. Charlie raised his glass and gave the man a grin. 'Good evening, sir. I guess the whole town is here tonight.'

Merriweather looked down at him as if he were some kind of talking bug. 'I don't think I've had the pleasure, sir,' he said, with more than a tinge of contempt.

'Indeed, the pleasure's mine,' Charlie said. 'Can I have the additional pleasure of buying you a drink?'

Merriweather held up his glass and examined it. He was grinning reflectively. 'I never like to deny a man pleasure,' he said, 'so I'll be pleased to accept your kind offer.'

He turned to the bartender. 'Give me a whiskey. I want the best, not that piss you dish out to your regular customers.'

The bartender gave Charlie a sly grin and poured out a glass of the best whiskey in the house.

'I see you're a man of taste,' Charlie observed.

Merriweather took a sip of his whiskey and gave a smile that was more like a sneer. 'So what do you want to know?' he asked Charlie.

Charlie shrugged. 'Why do you ask, my friend?'

Merriweather gave him a cursory glance. 'Nothing is free in this world, *mon ami*, so if a stranger buys a man a drink, it means he wants something. That's a law of nature. Don't you know that?'

'Well, I've picked up a few hints about how the world wags,' Charlie replied.

Merriweather turned to scrutinize him. 'You don't live in town, do you, my friend?'

'Well, I don't live anywhere in particular,' Charlie said. 'I just travel from place to place, helping out where I can.'

'You mean you're a drifter?' the man said.

'Some might say so,' Charlie replied. 'I would prefer the word healer.'

Merriweather raised an eyebrow and took a swig of his whiskey.

'And what about you, my friend?' Charlie said. 'I see you're toting a gun but you look like a professional of some kind.'

Merriweather was grinning now. He wasn't exactly friendly, but at least he looked a little more affable. 'I was indeed in a profession some years back, but like you I prefer the open range.' He nodded and drained his glass. 'Well, my friend, I must be on my way. Thanks for the drink; I'll see you around.' Then he turned and elbowed his way through the milling crowd towards the door, just as the performance was about to resume.

Charlie was looking for Kirk, but Kirk was nowhere to be seen. In fact he was outside under the ramada watching for Merriweather to appear, and he didn't have long to wait. The swing doors were thrust rudely aside and the man with the mutton-chop whiskers came striding out. Kirk stood in the shadows behind a wooden prop as Merriweather peered left and right as if to make sure he wasn't being observed. Then he went to the hitching rail, unhitched his horse, mounted up and rode out of town to the north.

'So, why didn't that mutton-chopped *hombre* stay for the second half of the show, and why did he ride into town in the first place?' Kirk asked himself. A strange, somewhat ugly suspicion began to form in his mind. 'And why did he ride north?' he wondered.

The swing doors opened and Charlie appeared. 'So, you're out here!' Charlie exclaimed. 'The show is about to begin again. Where's that mutton-chopped stuffed shirt?'

'He's just ridden off north.'

'Well, ain't that strange!' Charlie said.

'It is indeed,' Kirk agreed.

'You got any theories about that?'

'There are one or two ideas kicking around in my head.'

'You like to tell me about them?'

Someone rang a bell inside the hall. 'Let's go and watch the show,' Kirk said. 'I'll tell you later.'

They went inside and resumed their seats and Katie appeared from behind the curtain. She made a deep curtsey and struck a chord on that old honky-tonk piano. The crowd went mad and Kirk's heart turned over in his chest. 'What the hell's wrong with me?' he asked himself. 'Am I quite crazy with love?'

And then the thought struck him and it was so amazing that he gasped in horror.

'Are you OK?' Charlie asked him.

'No, but I've just had an idea!' Kirk replied.

'Well, what's wrong with having an idea? Even I get them once in a while.'

Black Bart and his two compadres were sitting with Alphonso and his buddies in an abandoned cabin not far north of River Fork. On the surface Black Bart and Alphonso were getting on well together. Mart had rustled up quite a tasty stew that the boys were tucking into with great relish.

'Well, Mart my man, you sure have a way with that cooking pan of yours. How did you learn those skills?' Alphonso asked.

Mart grinned with a degree of smugness. 'When you're out on the trail day and night you learn a whole heap of things.'

'Well, that's quite a gift,' Alphonso said, helping himself to another mug of stew. His table manners weren't exactly of the best but they were a whole lot more gentrified than Black Bart's, who slurped away like a grizzly sticking its nose into a pool of reed-covered water.

Steve was keeping watch outside when one of the horses snickered. He cocked his revolver and strained his eyes into the darkness. 'Who's there?' he said as the rider

70

emerged from between the cottonwoods.

'Don't get trigger happy,' the voice of Gus Merryweather came back as he rode up past the grazing horses and dismounted. 'You should be careful with that shooter of yours,' he said in a superior tone. 'You get a little nervous it might go off by mistake and blow a man's head off, you know that?'

'I don't make mistakes with a gun,' Steve snarled back. It was clear there was no love lost between the two men.

Gus Merriweather strode into the ruined cabin and sat down on a worm-eaten bench. 'Is there any of that fine-smelling stew left?' he asked.

Mart dipped a tin mug into what was left of the stew and handed it to him.

Merriweather regarded it with disdain. 'That's not enough to nourish a fly,' he said.

Mart grinned back at him. 'Sorry. That's all that's left.' He glanced briefly in Black Bart's direction.

Black Bart said, 'We thought you'd grab yourself something in town.'

'No time,' Merriweather said. 'I was too busy watching that divine creature tickling the ivories.' He gave a broad wink for Black Bart's benefit.

'So you saw the performance?' Alphonso said.

'Like I said,' Merriweather gave a somewhat sour grin. 'Didn't stay for the second half, though I was tempted to. A guy bought me a drink in the bar . . . best whiskey too. He wanted to know something, but I played kind of dumb.'

'So did you recognize him?'

Merriweather screwed up his face in thought. 'I didn't, but I had a strong feeling he knew why I was there.' He squinted at Black Bart. 'I've done what you asked me to

71

do, so what's the deal?'

'Well, it's all in my head. So I'll just lay it out before you.'

In the barn the performance was coming to an end and there was rapturous applause.

Charlie the Medic turned to his friend Adam Kirk. 'So what's this bright idea that's lit up in your brain?'

Kirk nodded. 'I'm still working on it, Charlie, but I figure that young woman is in great danger.'

Charlie showed no surprise. 'I believe you could be right on that,' he said. 'So what are we going to do about it?'

'Well, first I'm going to talk to her.'

Kirk was about to make his way towards the stage when he came face to face with Sheriff John Schnell.

'Well now, Adam Kirk, did you enjoy the show?' the sheriff asked him.

Kirk smiled. 'It was first class. I'm just going to congratulate the artists.'

John Schnell gave him a quizzical look. 'I saw your friend Charlie talking to that distinguished-looking stranger and I noticed the man didn't stay for the second part of the performance. Can you think why that was?'

'Well, I do have a theory about that. Why don't you talk to Charlie about it? He has a wise head on his shoulders.'

Schnell looked slightly surprised. Then he nodded. 'Indeed, I think I vill.'

Kirk went through to what served as a dressing-room, where John Smiley and Katie were relaxing.

'That was an excellent performance,' Kirk said.

'So you thought it went well?' John Smiley asked him.

'It went like a dream, even better than the shows in

72

Silver Spur,' Kirk said.

John Smiley nodded and smiled. 'Thanks for that, Mr Kirk.' He got up from his seat. 'I think I'll just go out and talk to some of the audience.' He almost winked at Kirk.

'Maybe I should come with you,' Katie said but before she could rise, Kirk said 'Please don't go, Miss Smiley, there's something I need to say to you.'

Katie looked at him closely. 'Is it something about the show?' she asked.

'Well, yes, indirectly,' he said. 'I didn't like to speak in front of your pa because I know he's a little hyped up at the moment since your brother . . .'

Katie held up her hand. 'Please don't mention that again,' she pleaded.

'I understand,' Kirk said. 'Perhaps this isn't the time, but I think I must speak.'

Kirk paused. How am I going to say this? he wondered. 'The fact is . . .' he said, 'certain things that have happened recently have led me to believe. . . .'

'To believe what?' she asked. She was staring at him unflinchingly. Or was it expectantly? He couldn't be certain.

He took a deep breath. 'The fact is I have come to believe you are in danger, Miss Smiley.'

Her eyes widened with surprise. 'In danger of what, Mr Kirk?'

Kirk wasn't quite sure how to continue. Speak straight out, he told himself. 'I think you are in danger of being kidnapped,' he said.

'Kidnapped! Why do you say that, Mr Kirk?'

Kirk shook his head and thought, I'm talking like an idiot. He said, 'What I mean is, I have reason to believe someone wants to capture you and hold you prisoner.'

Now her expression changed completely. 'Are you joking, Mr Kirk?' She was smiling sceptically.

'No, I'm deadly serious,' he said.

'Deadly!' She was almost laughing. 'That's an awful strong word, Mr Kirk!'

'Maybe the position is more serious than you realize, Miss Smiley,' he replied.

Katie shook her head. 'Why should anyone want to kidnap me?' she asked.

Kirk felt the blood pumping in his neck and he knew he was getting angry. 'Revenge,' he said. 'Revenge, Miss Smiley!'

Katie paused for a second. 'What do you mean?' she asked uncertainly. 'Who could possibly want to kidnap me for revenge?'

Kirk strove to calm herself. 'Not against you, Miss Smiley, but against your father.'

'But who would want to take revenge on my father, and for what?'

'Just think,' he said.

Suddenly her expression changed, and she said, 'You don't mean. . . ?'

Kirk nodded. 'Yes,' he said. 'The man you met on the trail, the big man with the black beard. He's the one your father out-boxed on the trail and who indirectly killed your brother. He's the one who robbed the bank here in River Fork and killed the bank manager, Andy. And he's the man whose face is on the wanted posters in the town jail. That's who I'm talking about, and that's the man I mean to bring to justice before he destroys anyone else's life.'

Katie saw that Kirk had become quite riled up and stared at him in amazement. 'Who are you, Mr Kirk?' she

74

asked him.

Kirk nodded and smiled. 'I'm Adam Kirk, a United States marshal, and I have two things in mind right now.'

'What two things?' she asked.

He took a deep breath. 'First, I'm going to bring Black Bart to justice. Second, I'm going to make sure he doesn't kidnap you.'

Katie suddenly looked serious. 'That's a really big deal, Mr Kirk,' she said. 'Is there anything else?'

'Yes, in fact there is . . .' and he raised his voice slightly: 'I'm going to ask you to marry me, Miss Smiley!'

CHAPTER SIX

'So what do we do?' Alphonso asked Black Bart the next morning.

'We grab the girl and then ride down to Silver Spur and rob the bank,' Black Bart told him.

Alphonso looked sceptical. 'Just like that?' he said with a grin.

'Well, if we plan it right, it shouldn't be too difficult,' Black Bart said.

'It's against the law to kidnap people, unless you hadn't noticed,' Merriweather remarked sardonically.

'Robbing banks is frowned upon somewhat too,' Alphonso put in. 'Anyway, why should you want to kidnap the girl? You figuring on ransom money?'

Black Bart shook his head and showed his rotting teeth. 'I don't want her for the dollars. I want her to warm my bed . . . and, well, a few other things besides.'

Everyone in the ruined cabin laughed so much the walls threatened to crack and burst apart.

'You going soft in the head?' Merriweather asked him.

Black Bart's face clouded over. 'Not so soft as you might think. I just might want to get even with that so-called entertainer John Smiley. I want to see him go yellow in the gills when he hears I've got his daughter in my care. I might even make him a granddaddy, who knows?'

There was more raucous laughter in the shack.

'I think you're plumb crazy,' Merriweather said.

Black Bart scowled. 'A man can't go on robbing banks for ever. You have to think about planning for the future. A man who looks ahead is a man with savvy.'

'Why don't we try the railroad?' Alphonso suggested. 'They say railroads are rich pickings. Even the James brothers have latched on to that one.'

'Well, that's a whole new territory,' Black Bart said. 'And I hear there's rich pickings in Silver Spur too.'

'Who told you that?' Merriweather asked him.

'Nobody told me. I just figured it out for myself.'

'So when do we start?' Steve the ex-waddy asked.

'No time like the present,' Black Bart growled.

'You mean today, right now?' Merriweather said with one eyebrow raised.

'Let's say we ride down there come sun-up tomorrow morning?' Black Bart said.

'What, the whole bunch of us?' Mart exclaimed.

A crafty grin spread across Black Bart's visage. 'I don't think that's the right way,' he agreed. 'If we ride into River Fork and start shooting up the place there could be a rumpus and some of us might even get ourselves killed.'

'So what is the nature of your plan?' Merriweather asked in a well pronounced tone that suggested Black Bart, like most politicians, had no plan at all.

Black Bart fixed a malevolent eye on him. He was never happy when someone questioned his plan or contradicted him. Indeed, one or two, like the bank manager, Andy, had ended up quite dead for that reason. 'What we do, is one of us, or maybe two of us ride into River Fork, pick up the girl and ride out again.'

Again there was ribald laughter in the cabin, and what was left of the windows rattled with mirth.

'*Pick up the girl?*' Alphonso exclaimed. 'You mean like picking blueberries off a bush?'

Black Bart was showing his decaying teeth again. 'We need to use our heads on this,' he said.

'You mean *you have to use your head?*' Merriweather said. 'That young woman plays those old ivories like an enchantress. She put a spell on the whole audience – and anyway, what harm has she done to you?'

Black Bart stared at Merriweather and growled like a bear looking at a man up a tree. 'You don't understand a thing, do you, Merriweather?'

Merriweather smiled right back at him. 'Oh, I understand a whole lot, Mr Bartholomew,' he sneered.

Both men seemed about to square off with one another. Black Bart was a whole lot heavier than Merriweather, but Merriweather was a whole lot smarter. So it was a dangerous moment.

Then Alphonso stepped in. 'Let's just calm down, gents, shall we?'

Merriweather held up his hand and grinned. 'Well, there's no need to get into a state of botheration, is there?'

Black Bart growled. But everyone knew he never forgave a man who crossed him.

'Well now,' Alphonso said, 'If we're going ahead with this scheme we have to decide how it is to be done.'

Everyone murmured in agreement, some with less enthusiasm than others.

'Well, boys, and who would you recommend to undertake that onerous task?' Merriweather asked, choosing words he knew Black Bart wouldn't understand or would resent if he did.

A heavy cloud seemed to pass over Black Bart's face. Then a ray of sunlight shone through. 'Well, Mr Merriweather, it could be you,' he suggested.

Merriweather grinned back. 'I'd like to oblige you, Mr Bartholomew, but I don't think that would be the best solution.'

'Why not?' Black Bart snapped.

'Well, several reasons spring to mind,' Merriweather said in a mocking tone. 'First, I'm not too eager to take unnecessary risks. Two, while I was in River Fork watching the performance, I happened to notice the sheriff was there with his good lady. And three, there was someone with them. . . .'

'So who would that be?' Black Bart asked him.

Merriweather ran his eyes over the whole company like President Lincoln about to address the troops at Gettisberg. 'That would be United States Marshal Adam Kirk,' he said.

There was a stunned silence.

'I wonder what he's doing in River Fork?' Alphonso asked.

'Whatever he's in town for I don't think it's too healthy for us,' Merriweather said. 'And there's another thing.' He paused again. 'A *hombre* I didn't know bought me a drink at the bar and I guessed he was a plant.'

'You mean like a pansy or a rose?' Mart joked from the other side of the table.

'No, not a pansy or a rose. More like poison ivy,' Merriweather said.

There was another silence as the words sank in.

'So you see,' Merriweather continued, 'I don't think I'm the man you're looking for. I'm not ready to stick my head in the noose . . . not quite yet, at least . . . not while I'm enjoying life so much.' He gave Black Bart a mocking glance.

Katie Smiley stared at Adam Kirk in astonishment. Was she dreaming or had he just proposed marriage to her. 'Are you asking me to marry you?' she asked.

Kirk smiled apprehensively. 'Indeed I am, Miss Smiley.'

Katie shook her head. 'You amaze me, Mr Kirk. First you warn me that I'm in danger of being kidnapped, and then you ask me to marry you! Can you be serious?'

'Indeed I am, Miss Smiley. Do you want me to get down on my knees and propose to you?'

'That won't be necessary, Mr Kirk,' she said with a smile that was not entirely discouraging.

'So what is your answer, Miss Smiley?'

She shook her head again. 'Well, Mr Kirk, I am truly honoured, but I'll need to think about that.'

Kirk nodded. His heart was beating so fast he thought, for the first time in his life, that he might actually pass out.

'Well now, boys,' Alphonso said diplomatically, 'since we've thrown in together I guess we should decide what's in the best interests of everyone concerned.'

'I agree with that,' Mart said.

'So, what do we do about the girl?' Steve put in.

'Well, I have a suggestion about that,' Merriweather said.

'And what is that?' Black Bart growled.

'With due respect to your thirst for revenge and your liking for that young filly, I suggest we ride down to Silver Spur first, and then think about the girl. After all, though they say money is the root of all evil it can be somewhat useful.' He glanced at Black Bart. 'Specially if you're hoping to retire and settle down with a good woman.'

That gave rise to more ribald laughter at Black Bart's expense, which didn't please him one little bit.

'That sounds like a good idea,' one of Alphonso's team piped up. He was Jasper Joseph, not known for expressing an opinion, though he was thought to be a reliable man in a tight corner. Even Black Bart was impressed.

'So you think we should do the bank in Silver Spur first?' he said.

Jasper Joseph looked thoughtful. 'Stands to reason, doesn't it? If we grab the girl first, all hell will break loose and the whole county will be looking for us, specially since you boys robbed the bank in River Fork.'

There was a murmur of agreement. 'That is so,' someone said.

Alphonso looked at Black Bart. 'What do you say to that, Bart? After the bank in Silver Spur nobody's gonna expect us to show up in River Fork again. So that will be the best time to get your revenge on that entertainer John Smiley.'

Black Bart scowled and looked as thoughtful as he could, which was somewhat unusual, to say the least. Then, after a moment, he shook his head. 'OK,' he agreed. 'For the time being justice can wait.'

Everyone looked relieved.

Black Bart looked round at the so-called team, 'Just as long as I get what I want in the end,' he growled.

It was around midnight, and most of the boys were sleeping in the ruined cabin or in their bedrolls under the stars. But Alphonso and Merriweather were out among the horses keeping a watchful eye out for anyone who might care to approach. Alphonso was by nature a cautious man, and he and Merriweather had ridden together for a number of years. Alphonso was smoking a curly pipe and Merriweather had a cigarillo clenched between his teeth.

'What do you think?' Alphonso asked Merriweather.

Merriweather chuckled quietly in the darkness. 'I think the guy's completely crazy, off his chump, and that indeed can be somewhat dangerous when it comes to decision making.'

Alphonso exhaled a haze of tobacco smoke against the moon. It was a really fine night for smoking and talking. 'So what do you think we should do about him?' he asked.

Merriweather chuckled again. 'What I think we should do is string him along, and use him to suit our own purposes.'

'I agree,' Alphonso said. 'So what did you really think after you'd been to River Fork to look things over?'

Merriweather took out his cigarillo and examined the ash on the tip. 'I think we're in a mighty dangerous business here, and if we're not careful we might get ourselves killed.'

'On the other hand we could get ourselves a fistful of dollar bills, maybe enough to ride away into the sunset and live like English lords,' Alphonso said.

'That may be so,' Merriweather agreed. 'But only if we play our cards right.'

'Sure,' Alphonso said, 'but that means you have to be less sassy with the man. Your trouble is you're a damned sight too smart and you don't mind showing it.'

Merriweather was still bubbling with merriment. 'I'm afraid that's my nature, my friend. It's a curse I have to live with. If I'm smarter than the people I meet with I have to show it. And if they outsmart me I give them my respect even if I have to kill them later.' He turned to Alphonso and grinned in the moonlight. 'And that *hombre* who bought me a drink of good whiskey in River Fork was no slouch. I almost took to him even though I might need to shoot him later.'

'You think it might come to that?'

Merriweather shrugged. 'Depends which way the dice rolls, doesn't it?'

At that moment Steve was behind a cottonwood tree taking a leak not far from the two men. He heard the murmur of conversation and crept closer behind the horses to hear what they were saying. Although he didn't hear a lot of what was said, he heard enough to arouse his suspicions. So he adjusted his pants and backed away quietly to where Mart was snoring close by. He thought about waking Mart, but decided to turn in again and wait until later. He had a lot to think about.

John Smiley was sleeping in the wagon and his daughter Katie was lying in her cot eight feet away. Her thoughts were far from sleep. She was thinking about two things: Adam Kirk's offer of marriage, and his warning that she was in danger.

At that moment John Smiley stirred, then he rose and sat on the edge of his cot.

'So you're awake?' Katie said quietly.

'Sure, I'm awake. Couldn't sleep,' he said, though a moment before he had been purring away.

'I need to talk to you,' Katie said.

'Well, I guessed you would some time or other,' he responded. 'And it always comes sooner than you expect.'

That wasn't as particularly good start. 'I need to talk to you seriously,' she insisted.

'Of course,' he conceded.

'So you know what I wanted to say?'

'Well, I have many gifts.' She could hear the smile in his voice. 'But one of them isn't mind-reading.'

Katie swung out of her cot. 'Adam Kirk asked me to marry him!' she said abruptly.

John Smiley cackled to himself. 'Didn't you expect it?' he asked.

'Well, yes, I believe I did,' she answered almost to her own surprise.

John Smiley was nodding sagaciously in the semi-darkness. 'And did you say yes?'

'I didn't say yes and I didn't say no,' she replied. 'I told him I'd think it over.'

There was a moment's silence. 'Seems a decent man,' he said as if to himself. 'He's helped us out of a few scrapes.'

'Did you know he's a United States marshal?'

Her father was nodding. 'I didn't exactly know, but let's say I'm not surprised.'

'He must be at least ten years older than me,' she ruminated.

'I guess so. That's young to be a US marshal, isn't it?'

'So, what do you think?'

'It's not for me to think; it's for you to think. Matrimony is a big step in a girl's life. What you've got to ask yourself is, do I care for the man, and will he make a good husband and father?'

Sound advice, Katie thought, but not particularly helpful, especially as John Smiley hadn't been the best of fathers himself. 'You know what this means, don't you?' she asked.

'I've been thinking about that,' he said.

'And what are your conclusions?' she asked.

John Smiley sat on his cot and said nothing for a while. It was as though he had fallen asleep just sitting there. 'Well now,' he said, 'what it means is far-reaching. Being a United States marshal is not being an entertainer. So Mr Kirk couldn't be expected to fit in with the show business. He's not that kind of man.'

'That is true,' she said deliberately. 'So, are you saying the show might have to come to an end?'

'Not necessarily,' he said. 'But I might have to consider following a lonesome trail.'

'How could you do that?' she asked him. 'You don't play the piano, do you?'

'I can strike out a chord or two, but nowhere near as good as you,' he said. 'That comes from your ma.'

They both lapsed into a meditative silence for a while.

'Well, I'll just have to think about it, won't I?' she said.

John Smiley neither agreed nor disagreed. He lay down in his cot and appeared to go back to sleep.

Katie lay down and pulled the bedcovers right up to her ears, but she couldn't sleep. A kaleidoscope of thoughts were spinning round in her head.

Steve was lying under the stars, trying to get his thoughts together. He had heard Alphonso and Merriweather go back into the broken-down cabin, but he couldn't sleep. The conversation he had heard troubled him deeply.

After about an hour when he could see the sky beginning to lighten in the east he heard Mart stir close by. 'Are you awake, buddy,' he said quietly.

'Just had a weird dream,' Mart replied.

'Don't think about weird,' Steve hissed. 'Think about real.' Then he told Mart about the conversation he had overheard down by the horses.

'Well, I'm not surprised,' Mart said. 'I always knew those two stuck-up pinheads were as slimy as the devil himself. You could hear it in their high-toned voices. I wouldn't trust either of those guys with two tin bits. They're both as slippery and poisonous as rattlers.'

'So what do we do about it?' Steve asked.

'What do you suggest, *amigo*?' Mart said.

Steve was thinking about the dollars Black Bart was holding for them after the robbery in River Fork and which he had not yet doled out. But he was also thinking about something else. 'Black Bart is too trigger happy for my taste,' he said. 'I didn't like the way he shot the bank manager in River Fork, and I didn't like the way he gunned down on those guys fishing in the creek. He wanted to kill those guys. . . . Another thing, there's a price on his head, and the guy's a born-again killer and that's a fact.'

'All that might be true,' Mart whispered. 'The question is, what do we do about it?'

Steve thought for a moment. 'What we could do,' he suggested, 'is cut our losses, roll up our bedrolls, get on our horses and ride out of here.'

There was a reflective silence.

'Where would we go?' Mart asked. 'If we ride out of here we'd ride out without a tin nickel to our names. Not only that, we're both wanted for bank robbery ourselves.'

A thoughtful silence came between them, but the clandestine conversation had come a little too late: the sun was already raising its head above the tree tops like a bright yellow, fried egg yoke. It would be a good day for action, but what kind of action; at that point neither of them could be sure.

*

It was sun-up, and Adam Kirk and Charlie the Medic were already out on Main Street. Charlie had eaten a hearty breakfast of flapjacks and good coarse toasted rye bread, and a plentiful supply of syrup, too. But he noticed that Kirk had just toyed with his food.

'You off your tucker?' he asked Kirk.

'I just don't feel hungry,' Kirk said absently.

'I guess you've got something on your mind,' Charlie the Medic said. 'But a man needs to start the day with something good under his belt. Otherwise he's fit for nothing much at all. So what's on your mind? Could it be that girl that's driving you crazy?'

'Maybe, just a little,' Kirk admitted to his friend.

Charlie grinned. 'A bit more than just a little,' he surmised. 'And did you slide the question towards her?'

'Yes, I did.'

'And what was her response?'

'She slid it right back to me.'

Charlie gave a murmur of laughter. 'Never knew you to be lovesick before, my friend. What the hell's got into you? Katie's a mighty fine young woman, but maybe she's not for you.'

Kirk nodded. 'You could be right.'

'Just like breaking in a wild bronco mare,' Charlie said. 'If she likes you she'll pacify down and come right back to eat out of your hand sooner or later.'

Kirk grinned. 'You should know, Charlie, the number of women you've had.'

'That's a long story,' Charlie said, 'and one I don't aim to bore myself with now.'

'OK, boys,' Black Bart said in his usual demanding tone. 'We've had our chuck. I guess it's a good day to have us some fun. So let's get ourselves on the trail and ride down to Silver Spur. I have a hunch there's gonna be one hell of a lot of dollars in the bank down there just ripe for the picking.'

'That's as maybe, but just how do we do the picking?' Jasper Joseph asked him.

Black Bart looked at the little squirt of a man with disdain. 'Why don't you leave the thinking to the big guys? I've got it all figured out. What we do is ride through the hills above the trail so we can keep an eye out. Then we put down camp within grabbing distance of Silver Spur and rest up till morning. Then come sun-up tomorrow we bust the bank down there and ride off into the distant hills never to be seen again.'

'Sounds like a fairytale,' Merriweather mocked. 'So why don't you tell us the rest of the plan right now? After all, we're all in this together, I believe.'

'And what about the sheriff down there?' Alphonso said. 'Name of Jack Kincade. I hear he's no pushover. Could be quite a handful in fact.'

Black Bart gave a snarl of contempt. 'When did you last see Kincade? He should have handed in his star a century ago. He's got the rheumatics so bad he can't hardly get his leg over his horse, not to mention anything else!'

Most of the bunch guffawed, but Steve and Mart exchanged uneasy glances.

At that moment Sheriff John Schnell of River Fork was drafting out a message to his friend Jack Kincade.

Good morning, there, Jack. I hope you and your folk are well on this beautiful morning. We're all doing fine up here. Just been enjoying the John Smiley show. That young woman strides the keyboard just like she's bin doing it for a hundred years or more. But that's beside the point. While we were watching the show Adam Kirk noticed a tall, neatly dressed gent he hadn't seen before. Looked like he was a lawyer or something, except he was wearing a gun by his side. Charlie the Doc stood the guy a drink to find out more and the strangest thing is the guy left after the first half of the show. Don't want to trouble you but I thought you should be informed, specially after the recent bank robbery up here.

Your good friend,

John.

Jack Kincade was sitting in Bridget's Diner when the message came through. His wife Bridget was busy serving her customers, among them the immense figure of Tiny Broadhurst who had just ordered a second portion of the pie he adored. Tiny raised his head from his pie momentarily and glanced at Kincade. 'See you got a wire through, Jack,' he said in his unusually high-pitched tone that sounded like a corncrake in a field near at hand.

'That's right, I did,' John Kincade agreed. He was remarkably tolerant of Tiny Broadhurst, who irritated almost everyone in Silver Spur with his bragging about how he had won the recent war almost single-handed.

'I guess it came from Sheriff Schnell up in River Fork, am I right?' Tony had gobbets of pie on his chops and down his shirt front. Kincade wondered how his wife, who kept herself well out of sight, could put up with him.

'Any trouble brewing?' Tiny enquired.

'I guess we'll have to see, won't we?' Jack Kincade replied.

After Tiny Broadhurst had left Bridget's Diner and gone across Main Street to lean on the bar in the saloon and drink himself even sillier than usual, Bridget said to her husband, 'So you got a wire from John Schnell?'

'Yes, I did,' he replied, 'And I don't know what to make of it. Maybe you should read it for yourself.' He handed her the paper and Bridget read the message. She was a shrewd woman, and her husband had always appreciated her advice; she had the uncanny knack of hitting on the truth. She read a few words out loud: ' . . . "the guy left after the first part of the show." Now I wonder why that would be.'

Jack Kincade looked at his wife and smiled. 'I think you might have something there,' he said. He read through the message again, and one phrase hit him right between the eyes: 'Looked like he was a lawyer or something, except he was wearing a gun by his side.' For some reason the description started a bell ringing in his mind.

CHAPTER SEVEN

Black Bart and the rest of the bunch were riding high in the hills above the trail from River Fork to Silver Spur. Black Bart was leading the way, but he felt deeply suspicious. He leaned towards Steve who was riding beside him, and spoke in an unusually quiet tone. 'Listen, Steve, we've bin riding together for quite a piece and you know how the dice roll. Tell me something: do you trust those high-flown talkers, Alphonso and Merriweather?'

Steve grinned and glanced back over his shoulder. 'Tell you the truth, boss man, I don't trust them any more than I would trust a bull with its horns down hoofing up the dust.'

Black Bart chuckled quietly to himself. 'You said that real good, my man. You said it real good. But don't keep looking back like that in case they get kind of suspicious.'

'What d'you want me to do?' Steve asked him.

'Just keep your eye out and your shooter handy in case they get a little out of line. Those two gents would shoot a man in the back just as quick as they'd shoot their own grandmother. You know that?'

Steve certainly knew it. He also knew that Black Bart

would do exactly the same if there were enough dollars involved.

Steve was in two minds. True, he had ridden with Black Bart for five years or more, which claimed some degree of loyalty. On the other hand, he'd seen Bart go downhill quite steeply when it came to killing other men. Killing other killers was one thing, but killing bank managers and honest fishermen was another thing altogether. Steve was as keen to find his pot of gold as anyone else on the frontier, but he had no wish to dangle at the end of a rope before he found it. He had a vivid imagination and the thought of swinging by the neck kept him awake nights. So he was in something of quandary.

Steve wasn't the only one in a quandary. Adam Kirk was trying to come to a decision too. On the one hand he wanted to make certain that Katie Smiley was safe. On the other hand, he was trying to figure out where Black Bart would strike again because, sure as the sun rose and sank every day, Black Bart would strike somewhere and soon!

'What's your next move?' Charlie the Medic asked him. Charlie was somewhat uneasy. He hadn't seen his *compadre* so restless and uncertain since they had teamed up together.

The day before, Kirk had talked to John Smiley again.

'Did you strike lucky?' John Smiley had asked him.

'What's lucky?' Kirk replied.

Smiley raised his head and looked up at the ceiling. 'You know what lucky is,' he said. 'Did that young lady accept your proposal?'

'Well, she didn't reject it.'

'What does that mean?' John Smiley looked sort of cagey.

'It means she doesn't know which way to go. She's considering her options. If she accepts my offer, it might mean the end of your entertainment business.'

That struck a resonating chord. John Smiley didn't look exactly surprised: he looked quizzical. 'You could be right,' he said. Kirk saw a look of defeat in his usually bright eyes. 'Maybe I should think about retirement. We have a spread back in Missouri, you know.' His eyes seemed to light up again. 'And how about you? Being a United States marshal has its complications, one of them being you're constantly on the move. And bad men take shots at you from time to time.'

Kirk had always been dedicated to the idea of good triumphing over evil, but he was a realist and he didn't buy into all that Saint George and the Dragon stuff. As a young man he had run away to sea, but had soon got tired of the confinement on board ship. Then he had joined the army and risen to the rank of sergeant, but that didn't satisfy him either. That's how he had become a US marshal, which left him free for a lot of the time. During his travels he had met Charlie the Medic who had dropped out of medical school and taken to the road.

'I guess we're just a couple of tumbleweeds drifting along through the desert of life,' Charlie the Medic said philosophically. But Kirk figured even tumbleweeds have to lodge somewhere and put down roots eventually.

'OK,' Charlie the Medic said to him. 'I've made up my mind. I'm going to ride down to Silver Spur and talk to the doc down there. He might even take me on as his assistant. I might not be fully qualified but I know how to bind up wounds and fix folk up well enough. After a little time I might even go back east and apply for medical school again.' He looked sideways at his *amigo*. 'Maybe we should follow our noses – you stay up here in River Fork and I ride down to Silver Spur. Give you a chance to go on with your wooing, and me to come to a decision on my future as a possible sawbones.'

Adam Kirk was thinking on the matter. He wondered if it were possible that Katie Smiley might eventually weaken and take pity on him. He dug out a coin and held it up. 'I'm going to spin this coin, and if it comes down head up I'll stay right here. But if it comes head down, I'll give up my quest and ride down to Silver Spur with you.'

Charlie gave a wry smile. 'So you'll give up the girl of your dreams just on the toss of a coin?'

Adam Kirk grinned. 'That's not exactly what I said. Maybe I should let Katie Smiley think on the matter for a while.'

'I see. You mean like the saying "absence makes the heart grow fonder"?'

'I don't think that's what I said either,' Kirk responded.

'Why don't you spell it out? I'm just a simple half-baked medic. I never studied deep thinking at school.'

Kirk pulled his face into a half smile. 'What I think is, if a thing's going to happen, it's going to happen whatever you plan.'

'That sounds sort of fatalistic to me. So you mean it's written in the stars?'

'Not exactly,' Kirk said. 'What I think I mean is, that when a thing's happened, it's happened and there isn't a darned thing you can do to change it.'

Charlie grinned. 'Well, that's a deal too heavy for my poor brain to handle. So why don't you just spin the coin, because it won't make any difference either way.'

Kirk spun the coin.

*

John Smiley was sitting with his daughter Katie in the saloon. He was shifting uneasily in his chair and twiddling his thumbs, a sure sign that he was trying to come to a decision. Katie looked at him and smiled, though in fact she felt deeply unsettled. 'Why are you doing that twiddling?' she asked him.

'Doing what?' he said.

'Twiddling your thumbs like that.'

John Smiley looked down and stopped twiddling. 'I was trying to work things out.'

'And have you come to any conclusions?' she asked.

'Well, I have come to a conclusion,' he said. 'And that is, you're just like your ma. You come straight out with it.'

Katie was smiling. 'Well, someone has to say things as they are around here.'

John Smiley came right back. 'In that case why don't you tell me how you feel about that young man who has asked you to marry him?'

Katie nodded. 'And what if you tell me your plans for the future? It seems to me that they're both part of the same problem.'

The coin came down head down, and both Kirk and Charlie looked at it with interest.

'OK,' Kirk said with a grin. 'The gods have spoken; I ride to Silver Spur with you.'

Charlie the Medic might have been secretly pleased, but he didn't smile. 'Well, I hope you don't come to regret it,' he said.

Kirk nodded. 'When a man takes up the plough he must plough a straight furrow and never look back.'

'Another of your wise saws,' Charlie said, 'but don't forget that when he gets to the end of the patch he turns and ploughs back in the other direction.'

Kirk smiled. 'You know, Charlie, I reckon you're a hell of lot wiser than you claim to be.'

John Smiley gave a deep sigh. 'OK,' he said, 'I've come to a decision.'

'And what may that be?' Katie asked him with a cautious grin.

'Well,' he said after a dramatic pause. 'I think I shall give up my travels and head back home to Missouri.'

'Is that what you really want?' she asked.

'That's what I plan to do,' he replied. 'When I get home I shall start a theatre group in the barn. I dreamed about it last night, and it was so vivid I could have stretched out my hand and touched the stage. I was also talking to two of the actors, and they might just as well have been as real as you and me.'

'That sounds like a wholesome dream,' she said. 'And that's helped to gather my thoughts as well.'

John Smiley looked almost mischievous. 'Really, my dear, and what have you decided to do?'

'I shall come with you and settle down on the farm.'

'And is that what you really want?' he asked.

'That's what I've decided,' she said, a little too decisively, he thought.

'Well, in that case we'll head for Silver Spur come sun-up,' he said. The trail led through Silver Spur towards their home in Missouri.

Black Bart and his team were now by the river where they had taken pot shots at those unfortunate fishermen; from here it was a short ride to Silver Spur.

'This is where we rest up,' he said. 'We can light a fire

and cook up a meal. Mart's a really a good hand at that, and you can all tank up and sleep easy in your bedrolls. Then come sun-up we can ride down to Silver Spur and do the bank job.' He chuckled in anticipation.

'So how do we do the bank job?' Alphonso asked him.

'Well, listen up and I'll tell you,' Black Bart said. He had perched his huge bulk on a log facing the river, and he chuckled to himself as he remembered the earlier scene with the fishermen. 'You recall what happened, Steve?' he said. 'The way those two yellow bellies scrambled for the shore when I shot up their canoe? They looked just like two ducks flapping their wings. I could have taken them out, but I was too busy laughing to aim straight. Otherwise we could have had ourselves a bowl of duck soup!' Black Bart roared with loud raucous laughter. It was so loud it might have been heard as far as Silver Spur and beyond.

In fact it was indeed heard, and the men who heard it were squatting in the bushes no more than two hundred feet away. They were the very fishermen Hank Holden and Jess Jessimore whom Black Bart had shot up earlier, and they were in fact hoping to shoot one or two ducks.

'Well, I'll be damned!' Jesse Jessimore hissed to his son-in-law. 'That's the very guy who tried to shoot us up.'

Hank Holden raised his spyglass and peered across the river. 'Well, so it is!' He focused on the camp. 'But lookee here! There were three of them then, and now I see seven. So they must have teamed up with another bunch. I just wonder what they have in mind.'

'Well, whatever it is it can't be good for our health, or anybody else's for that matter,' Jess Jessimore said. 'So what do we do?'

'Well, one thing's for sure,' Holden said. 'That big man has a price on his head, dead or alive for murder, and we could be in line for the reward if we play our cards right.'

'You don't mean we take a pop at him right now?' Jess Jessimore said in surprise.

'Not if you want to keep your scalp and collect those dollars.'

'So what do we do?'

'Common sense tells me we ride back to Silver Spur and tell the sheriff where they're holed up.'

'That sounds like a very good idea,' Jess Jessimore agreed, 'but maybe we should move closer first and listen. That big man has an awful loud mouth and we might learn something to our advantage.'

So they edged back into the trees and moved a little closer. Because of the flow of the river and the distance they couldn't hear clearly, but what they did hear made their hearts beat a whole lot faster and helped them to decide on their next move. Black Bart's voice boomed out loud and clear, and the words the eavesdroppers heard most loudly were 'Silver Spur' and 'a heap of greenbacks'!

'Well, boys, this is how it will pan out,' Black Bart was saying. 'We divide up and ride into Silver Spur. Four of us ride down Main Street and attract attention.'

'Hold on, there!' Alphonso Sebastian said. 'What do you mean, "attract attention"? Are you suggesting we blow kisses to the womenfolk and raise our hats to the gentlemen?'

This gave rise to guffaws of laughter, which made Black Bart's face cloud over. 'You know damn well what I mean!' he roared. 'There's serious greenbacks involved here!'

'OK,' Jacob Merriweather intervened. 'Why don't you just spill it out, Bartholomew? Tell us how we attract attention, and who's going to do it. And what the rest of the bunch do.'

'Yes, well I've thought about that, too,' Black Bart said. He closed his eyes momentarily, as though trying to picture the scene in his head was quite painful. 'Why don't you, Alphonso, and two of your bunch go into the store and get yourselves into a skirmish of some kind.' He turned to Steve: 'And why don't you go with them, Steve? You're good at handling steers.'

There was a momentary pause and then they all laughed again, except for Black Bart, who scowled. Humour had never been his strongest attribute.

'OK. So what about the rest of us?' Jacob Merriweather asked him. 'What do we do?'

Black Bart showed his rotten teeth in a broad grin. 'Well, as soon as Alphonso and his bunch have attracted attention, the rest of us walk right into the bank and fill our sacks with greenbacks.'

Merriweather twitched his whiskers. 'Just like that?' he said.

'Well, we might have to do a little persuading.' Black Bart was still showing his blackened stumps.

'You mean at the end of a gun?' Mart said.

'Well, that's part of the deal,' Black Bart replied, 'but think of all those greenbacks. When we've finished this job we can light out and head west, to California or Oregon, somewhere where they grow big juicy oranges and we can sit in rocking-chairs and enjoy the sun all day.'

'And how d'you figure we divvy out the greenbacks?' Alphonso Sebastian asked, adjusting his wire-framed specs like an English lord.

'Fair and square,' Black Bart said, 'fair and square.'

It took Jesse Jessimore and his son-in-law no more than an

hour to ride back to Silver Spur once they got clear of the scrub by the river. Their wives hadn't been at all pleased by their duck-shooting escapade, especially after the last incident during which they almost got themselves killed, but they both figured that boys will be boys, so they had turned a blind eye.

When Jesse and Hank rode into town at around midnight they didn't head for home and their wives: they went right to Bridget's diner and rapped on the door, which was locked. Bridget and her assistant were clearing the tables and washing the dishes, and Sheriff Kincade was nowhere to be seen.

When the two men rapped impatiently on the door Bridget was none too pleased. But she unlocked the door and peered out. 'What do you want at this time of night?' she demanded.

'Where's the sheriff?' Hank Holden shouted.

'The sheriff is where all good people should be. He's upstairs getting ready for bed. And keep your voices down. The kids are abed and I don't want them disturbed.'

'I'm real sorry,' Jesse said, 'but we need to see the sheriff right now because there's gonna be a big commotion in town.'

Bridget still looked doubtful, but suddenly Jack Kincade intervened. 'So, what happened?' he asked the two scared-looking men.

'Well, we were up by the river hoping to shoot one or two ducks,' Jesse Jessimore said, 'but before we could fire a shot. . . .'

But then Hank suddenly interrupted: 'The long and short of it is, we saw Black Bart.'

Jack Kincade narrowed his eyes. 'OK, boys, maybe you should tell me about it.' He turned to his wife. 'I'll just go across to my office and hear what these two boys have to say.'

Jack Kincade sat behind his desk and looked up. His policy was to listen quietly to everything that was said without getting unduly excited, because in his opinion an excited man is a vulnerable man. 'Now, boys, tell me your story.'

'It ain't no story, it's God truth!' Jesse Jessimore said.

'OK, Pa,' his son-in-law put in. 'Why don't you let me tell the sheriff like it happened?'

'Why don't you do that?' Jack Kincade leaned forwards and rested his elbows on his desk. 'Go ahead, Mr Holden.'

Early next morning Adam Kirk and Charlie the Medic were on the trail riding towards Silver Spur. Charlie had enjoyed an ample breakfast and he was in no mood to complain about anything except that he'd seldom seen Kirk looking so downbeat before.

'Well, my *amigo*, if you don't pull yourself out of this morbid state of mind, you'll be so downbeat you'll fall right off your horse and lie face down on the trail waiting for the buzzards to peck at you, you know that?'

Kirk looked at him sideways and grinned. 'You sure know how to cheer a man's spirits. You should be with Saint Peter shaking the stiffs by the hand as they enter the Pearly Gates.'

Charlie chortled with laughter. 'That's a great idea, *mon ami*, except I don't think they allow six guns up there. I understand they're very particular about that.'

Kirk grinned again. 'That's OK. I'm a little short on shells at the moment.'

'So, why are you riding to Silver Spur with me?' Charlie asked him.

'For two reasons, I guess. I want to see the doc there.'

Charlie nodded. 'Well, Martin Buchanan is a very fine doctor, but I don't think he specializes in broken hearts. That's way out of his territory.'

Kirk smiled broadly which suited his face a lot better. 'Thought I might put in a good word for you,' he said, 'because I think you might have healing hands, my friend.'

The two *compadres* were about half way between River Fork and Silver Spur, and they were in no particular hurry. They aimed to reach Silver Spur in time for a bite of lunch in Bridget's Diner.

'And another thing. . . .' Kirk said.

'Well, I know that,' Charlie said. 'You told me about your hunch already.'

'That is so,' Kirk said. 'My hunch takes me towards Silver Spur. I don't know why and I don't know when. It's just that I can smell that *hombre* Black Bart from twenty miles around and I know he's not far from here. So before I reach the Pearly Gates I might need that six shooter you mentioned just now for a little law business.'

'Well, that's a distinct possibility.' Charlie the Medic had great respect for Kirk's so-called hunches. He looked up at the sky. 'Why don't we stop off here for a while and let the horses graze and drink. I believe there's a pool along here if I remember right.'

Kirk agreed. He was in no particular hurry to get to Silver Spur as long as they reached the town before sundown. So they turned off the trail and headed for the pool.

Kirk never smoked. He thought it was a foolish habit and a downright waste of hard-earned dollars. So he just squatted by the pool as Charlie the Medic lit up his pipe, took a puff or two, and looked as contented as a golden ass.

Suddenly Charlie looked at Kirk. 'You hear that, *mon ami?*'

'I hear it,' Kirk said. 'It sounds like a wagon rolling along.'

'You got a good ear,' Charlie said. 'I'll just take a looksee.'

He got up and peered between the branches and saw the wagon. 'That's John Smiley unless I'm a downright ass,' he said. 'Maybe I should go talk to him. There he sits behind his two horses, and I see Katie his daughter too. She's sitting there with him looking as fresh and beautiful as a flower in the forest. Shall I step out and hail them?'

Kirk was still squatting on his heels looking across the pool. 'Don't bother, *mon ami.* Let them pass.'

Charlie watched and listened until the wagon had rattled away towards Silver Spur. Then he came back and squatted beside Kirk where he inhaled and blew a cloud of blue smoke towards the distant trees. 'You know what?' he said quietly.

'What?' Kirk said.

'Bitterness never did anyone any good at all. Bitterness can kill a man.'

Kirk looked down at the water and saw bubbles from a fish popping on the surface. 'I'm sure you're right about that,' he said.

CHAPTER EIGHT

Sheriff Jack Kincade was sitting with his friend Doc Martin Buchanan in the doc's office. He had just told Doc Buchanan the story Hank Holden and his father-in-law Jesse Jessimore had told him. 'Now they've gone home to be beaten up by their wives,' he concluded with a smile.

'Well, those two boys might not be the brightest and the bravest but they've got good ears. So what are you going to do about it?'

Jack Kincade shrugged. 'I think I have to prepare for the worst but I don't want to panic the community. So I think I'll just stroll across to the bank and have a word with Mr Spalding. And you'd better stand by with your medical skills in case they're needed. It could be a long day.' Kincade hitched up his gunbelt and walked across Main Street to the bank.

The bank manager Cyril Spalding was sitting behind the counter in a white shirt with a somewhat oversized black bow tie and a belt and braces. He was one of the world's pessimists.

'Good day to you, Mr Spalding,' the sheriff said. 'I'd appreciate a word with you in private.' Fortunately, business was slack, so there was nobody else in the bank at that

104

moment except Nick Shamburg, the manager's assistant.

Spalding's face took on an earnest expression. 'You'd better come through to my office, Sheriff. Shamburg, look after the shop, will you?'

Shamburg, a youth with a red neck and pimples, sprang up from behind the counter. 'Why, yes certainly, Mr Spalding.'

They went through to the office, which was so small you couldn't have swung a mouse in it. Spalding sat behind his desk in the office and Kincade sat across from him.

'How can I help you, Sheriff?'

Kincade looked across and saw concern in the banker's eyes. 'I don't think you need to alarm yourself unduly, Mr Spalding. But I want to suggest you do something to assist me.'

'Of course.' Spalding looked hopeful but a little unsettled. He was a nervous man especially after the shooting to death of his fellow manager up in River Fork.

Kincade leaned forward. 'What I suggest is you close the bank for the day.'

Spalding's opened his eyes wide in astonishment. 'You want me to close the bank, Sheriff?'

'That's what I'm suggesting, Mr Spalding.'

'But why . . .' Spalding stammered . . . 'why should that be?'

Kincade cleared his throat. 'Let me tell you this in confidence. I've had news. My informants tell me that certain badmen are in the area.'

'Which badmen?' Spalding began to look more alarmed by the minute. Since the shooting up in River Fork he had hardly slept at nights. His wife had advised him to visit Doc Buchanan and ask for a sedative to help him sleep. 'And if those men come into the bank with their guns just give them the money and leave the rest to Sheriff Kincade,' she had said.

Good advice, though, perhaps, in the circumstances!

'What do I tell the customers?' he asked Kincade.

'Don't tell them anything. Just put up a notice: "Closed till tomorrow due to accounting business".'

Spalding struggled with his thoughts for a second or two. 'Very well, Sheriff, if that's what you advise, but my customers might not be too pleased.'

Jack Kincade nodded and stood up, and for some reason he held out his hand to the bank manager. Spalding looked at his hand with suspicion and then accepted it with his own fish-wet hand.

Jack Kincade stepped out on to Main Street and thought what a beautiful day it was. Not a cloud in the sky and as still as doom – that was the word that leapt into mind: doom!

He looked first right and then left. And he thought to himself, Bridget's damned right: I should hand in my badge and take up a more respectable business. Bridget's Diner was a successful business, so there'd be no problem there. It was just his own damned pig-stubborn nature that stopped him from retiring. I am as stubborn as a mule, he thought as he looked down Main Street.

When he turned he saw the enormous form of Tiny Broadhurst looming towards him. Tiny wasn't exactly Silver Spur's clown, but he certainly qualified as the town's best gossip monger. He knew everything people were doing almost before they knew it themselves!

'Hi, there, Sheriff Kincade!' he greeted in his unusually high-pitched tone.

'Good day to you, Tiny,' Kincade replied somewhat unenthusiastically.

Tiny Broadhurst squinted down at him. 'It's one mighty fine day,' he said. 'And I hope what I hear ain't to be credited.'

'That depends on what you hear,' Kincade replied.

'Oh, well . . .' Tiny grinned in a half bashful way. . . . 'You know what I mean. About that damned bad guy they call Black Bart.'

Kincade sighed. 'So you've been talking to Hank Holden and Jesse Jessimore?'

Tiny Broadhurst preened himself. 'Just happened to bump into them. Jesse is an old friend of mine, so it was sort of natural, weren't it?'

Kincade nodded. No more time for discretion: if Tiny knew Black Bart was in the area, everyone else would know, which was both an advantage and a disadvantage. An advantage because the sensible folk would keep their heads down; a disadvantage because some of the wilder bunch might come right out with old-style weapons and get themselves shot.

'But don't you worry, Sheriff,' Tiny crowed, 'Whatever you do, I'll be right behind you, cos you're gonna need an old soldier by your side.'

Kincade held his head on one side for a moment. 'Well, Tiny, my advice to that old soldier is go back into the saloon and lean on the bar as usual, because this is a situation I can handle by myself.'

Tiny grinned. 'Well, just give me a call if you need me.' He stared down Main Street towards River Fork. 'Why bless my boots and suspenders, here comes a wagon, and if my eyes are still keen it's my old friend John Smiley and his daughter Katie, a fine woman if ever there was one. Beautiful as a lily in spring.'

Kincade was still standing in the middle of Main Street

107

as John Smiley and his daughter Katie rode in their wagon towards him.

'Good day to you, Sheriff Kincade!' Smiley shouted in his melodious Thespian tone.

'Good day to you!' Kincade replied, and he doffed his Stetson to Katie, 'And to you, Miss Smiley.'

Katie bowed her head graciously in reply.

'Are you here to give us another of your performances?' Kincade asked.

'No, no, we're just passing through,' John Smiley said. 'We're on our way back home to Missouri.'

'Don't tell me you're giving up in your profession, sir?'

'On the contrary, we'll be starting up a theatre group right there in our own town.' John Smiley smiled with confidence.

Kincade saw that Katie Smiley looked somewhat less convinced, though she said nothing.

'So where will you be staying the night?' Kincade asked him.

'Oh, we'll just park ourselves behind the Long Branch Saloon as usual. My old friends Kev and Sophia will be pleased. Then come sun-up we'll be on our way to Missouri where my wife's sister has been holding fort until we return. She's a good woman and never had the fancy to marry. So I guess we'll get along real fine.'

Kincade looked at Katie again, but she just smiled and made no comment. Kincade stepped closer to the wagon. 'I think I should warn you, Mr Smiley, I've had news that Black Bart and his men have been seen between River Fork and here. So you'd be wise to keep your eyes peeled.'

'Well, thank you, Sheriff. I'll keep that in mind. And I've got my Peacemaker handy.' He patted his side where the six-shooter rested . . . 'Just in case we meet him on the trail. When you've been bitten by a rattlesnake, you make sure it doesn't happen again.'

'Well, don't get trigger happy, my friend, in case you shoot the wrong snake.'

John Smiley laughed. 'Well, *adios amigo.* See you around.' Then he whipped up the horses and the wagon trundled on towards the saloon.

Jack Kincade stepped across to his wife's diner where she and her assistant were already starting to serve the early customers.

Bridget said to him, 'Jack, you look kind of strained. Why don't you sit yourself down and rest?'

Jack sat down, but he felt far from restful. All eyes seemed to turn on him, eager for information. A farmer named Bradley, who rarely came to town, spoke in a loud voice. 'Is this right, Sheriff, what I hear?'

'Depends what you hear,' Jack said.

Bradley wasn't amused. 'I come in early to the bank and find it's closed. How come?'

'I'm sorry for any inconvenience,' Jack replied. 'The bank is closed at my request.'

Bradley scowled. 'Is it true that Black Bart has been seen close to town?'

'I believe so.'

'And what are we gonna do about it?'

'There's nothing much you can do, Mr Bradley, apart from keeping yourself out of the line of fire if he and his bunch show up.'

'Well, I didn't bring my shotgun with me, so I can't help much.'

'You don't need to help at all,' Kincade told him. 'The best thing you can do is keep your head low and let me do the rest.'

Kincade then went to his office and checked his gun store and made certain all the weapons were loaded and in good order. Then he sat behind his desk with his revolver on top and wrote up the day's events . . . so far. Though he had never been particularly fond of paperwork he always wrote up everything so the next incumbent would have a good account of the law in Silver Spur. *The next incumbent* he thought, with a chill in his spine as he put down his pen and looked through the window on to Main Street, where everything seemed to be proceeding much as usual – though maybe there were fewer folk about. Then he saw something that raised his spirits somewhat: Adam Kirk and Charlie the Medic were riding in from the direction of River Fork.

Jack Kincade rose from behind his desk and opened the door, just as Kirk and Charlie rode up to his office.

'Hi there, Sheriff!' Kirk said. 'Thought we'd just stop off and pay our respects.'

Charlie tipped his hat and smiled broadly. 'How you doing, Mr Kincade?'

Kincade said he was doing just fine, though deep down in the pit of his stomach he felt somewhat less than fine. In fact he had a creepy feeling he had learned to associate with fear. 'Why don't you gentlemen step right into the office if you're not too weary. I have one or two things I'd like to share with you.'

The two men dismounted and tethered their horses and walked into the office.

Kirk looked at Kincade and nodded. 'So you have something to share with us,' he said, looking at the revolver on Kincade's desk.

Kincade stared at him. 'I've had news about Black Bart,' he said. 'Two men from the town report seeing him and

110

his bunch up by the river towards River Fork. Apparently there were seven of them. I've asked the bank manager to close the bank for the day just in case.'

'Is that wise?' Charlie the Medic asked.

'I thought it best,' Kincade told him, 'but some folk are none too happy about the situation.'

Black Bart and the bunch were in the hills close to Silver Spur. Steve had looked down on the trail from River Fork to Silver Spur through his spy glass. 'Lookee here!' he said to his buddy Mart, 'I see two riders.'

'Two riders are just two riders,' Mart replied philosophically.

'Well, take a look, and tell me what you see.' He handed Mart his spyglass.

Mart peered through it: 'Well, I see two riders and. . . .' He paused with a gasp . . . 'unless I'm a blind man, one of those riders is US marshal Adam Kirk.'

'Give that to me!' Black Bart grabbed the spyglass and peered towards the trail. 'Well, I'll be damned!' he said. 'You're right, that is Marshal Kirk.'

Alphonso Sebastian adjusted his wire-rimmed specs and looked towards the trail. 'You know what this means, Bartholomew, don't you?'

'It could mean two things,' Black Bart said.

'And what might they be?' Jacob Merriweather asked with a nervous grimace.

'It might mean he's just passing through, or he's got wind of our plans.'

'Well, either way it doesn't sound too healthy to me,' Merriweather said.

Black Bart wrinkled his nose. 'Well, I guess it ain't too healthy for him because it gives me the chance to blast his head off.'

'As well as doing the bank?' Jacob Merriweather laughed.

'Are you boys yellow as chickens?' Black Bart roared. 'If needs be I'll ride in on my own and rob the bank and kill Adam Kirk in one swoop! You think I can't do that?'

'Well, you could try, I guess, if you're damned cussed enough. But I wouldn't try my luck if I were you,' Merriweather said, 'unless you want to find yourself lying face up in a wooden box, that is.'

Steve looked at Mart, and Mart raised an eyebrow.

After a moment a ray of sunshine seemed to light up in Black Bart's brain and he calmed down somewhat. 'Well then, boys,' he growled, 'what we do is we keep to our plan. The only difference is, we don't ride into Silver Spur today, we ride in first thing tomorrow when they'll all be busy eating their ham and eggs and stuff.'

Alphonso Sebastian looked at Jacob Merriweather and said. 'What do you think, boys? Shall we settle for that?'

Nobody said anything against the plan, so the matter was settled.

It was getting on towards sunset, and still there had been no sign of Black Bart and his bunch in Silver Spur. Cyril Spalding appeared in Jack Kincade's office and he was in a fluster. 'I've done what you suggested,' he said to Jack Kincade, 'but nothing happened except the bank has lost a lot of business. I put a wire through to Head Office and the bosses are none too pleased. If we don't open tomorrow morning, my head will be on the line.'

'Well, I apologise, Mr Spalding,' Kincade said, 'but your head will be on the line even more if Black Bart and his bunch decide to rob the bank.'

Spalding started to blink furiously. 'So what are you going to do?' he demanded.

'What I'm going to do is offer you the full protection of the law, but I can't guarantee everything.' He paused. 'But I do have one ace in the hole in the shape of US marshal Adam Kirk.'

A glimmer of relief appeared in Spalding's eye. 'So will it be all right to open for business tomorrow morning?'

Kincade nodded. 'That's for you to decide. We'll give you all the protection we can.'

Adam Kirk and Charlie the Medic were in Bridget's Diner enjoying an excellent dinner. Bridget had agreed to accommodate them as long as they stayed in Silver Spur. As usual she was worried about her husband.

'He gets himself all wound up. He doesn't show it, but I see the signs,' she said. 'He's over there in his office, fretting and worrying in case those desperate men come riding into town, and all because of those two gossipmongers Jesse Jessimore and his son-in-law Hank. Those boys have never done an honest day's work in their lives. They're just a couple of bums.'

'Well, don't you fret yourself, Mrs Kincade,' Charlie said reassuringly. 'If those bully boys ride into town they'll be sure of a hot reception.' He got up from the table and patted his mouth with a paper napkin. 'That was a truly delicious meal. If you'll excuse me, I'm going to walk over to the Long Branch Saloon and see what news I can pick up.' He winked at Adam Kirk.

Bridget looked across at Adam Kirk. 'I'm real glad you're here, Mr Kirk. My husband needs all the support he can get. His friend Doc Buchanan is real worried about him, what with the rheumatics and all.'

Charlie the Medic paused on Main Street to look up at

113

the twinkling stars. According to the natives those stars are the campfires of the ancestors, he thought. Of course, I don't believe any such nonsense, but it's a beautiful fantasy; the alternative gives me the creeps!

The saloon was crowded as usual, but he noticed one person in particular – John Smiley, who looked at him and smiled.

'Take a drink with me,' Smiley offered. Charlie perched on a stool beside him. Kev, the owner of the Long Branch, came over and poured Charlie a beer. Charlie noticed that John Smiley was drinking a pale liquid that looked suspiciously like water. 'You drying out?' he asked.

'Trying to keep on the rails,' John Smiley replied. 'My girl Katie told me I should stop drinking after that unfortunate incident up in River Fork.'

'So where are you headed?' Charlie asked him.

'Back to Missouri, where I aim to set up my own theatre business. When a man's got to stop, a man's got to stop, you know that?'

'I've been thinking on the same lines myself,' Charlie told him.

'But we're not pushing on until after the fireworks.'

'Fireworks!' Charlie echoed wryly. 'This is isn't China. Here the firecrackers are bullets, and bullets can hit you right in the heart or the head and kill you.'

John Smiley turned to him and grinned. 'That's why I'm wearing my hogleg.' He reached down and tapped the revolver at his side.

Charlie shook his head. 'I don't think you should use that gun. Your girl Katie needs you alive and healthy.'

John Smiley took a sip of his water and said: 'Mr Charlie . . . excuse me, I never heard your given name. . . .'

'You can cut the Mister. Charlie will do nicely.'

114

'Well, Charlie, I used to work in a shooting gallery when I was young, so I know well enough how to shoot. And I promised myself that if I met that fat slug who killed my boy I'd take revenge on him. So I hope he rides into Silver Spur real early. If we come face to face I aim to shoot him dead.'

'D'you think Katie agrees with that?'

John Smiley looked somewhat sheepish. 'She doesn't have to. Katie's a damned sight too soft-hearted.'

'Where is she right now?' Charlie asked him.

'I guess she's out back somewhere yattering with Kev's good lady.'

'Well, don't drink too much of that *water* in case you turn into a fish.'

Adam Kirk was sitting with Jack Kincade in the back room of Bridget's Diner. They were talking about the next morning.

'So Black Bart didn't come in after all,' Kirk said. 'How do you figure that?'

Kincade pondered the matter. 'That huge chunk of shit may be stupid but he's as cunning as a wolf. Maybe he thought first light would be better, for some reason.'

'Another reason could be he lost his grip.'

Kincade raised his eyebrows and nodded. 'Well, you could be right at that. Those two fishermen might not have heard what they thought they heard.'

'So what do we do, come sun-up?' Kirk asked him. 'This is your patch and I'm here to help.'

Kincade didn't have time to answer because at that moment Bridget came in with Charlie the Medic.

'What's doing in the Long Branch?' Kirk asked Charlie.

'What's doing is John Smiley is propping up the bar and drinking something that looks suspiciously like water, and

115

he's packing a gun, too. He's got wind of the fact that
Black Bart's been seen in the area, and he wants him
dead.'

Kirk looked thoughtfully at the table and then at
Charlie. 'Did you see Katie?'

'I believe Katie was out back talking to Kev's good lady,
but I didn't see her. Smiley told me they were on their way
to Missouri where he hopes to set up in the theatre business.'

'Well, let's hope they make it,' Bridget said.

'You boys better get your heads down real tight,' Black
Bart said in his usual strident tones, 'because tomorrow's
the big day and I don't aim to let any man stop me.'

'Or woman either,' Jacob Merriweather interjected.

'Well, you're right at that,' Black Bart said with a
fiendish grin.

They were camped on a bluff not far from Silver Spur.
In fact they could look down and see the twinkling lights
of Silver Spur in the not-too-far distance.

Mart had cooked up quite a respectable meal from the
scraps he had available, which didn't amount to much.
Steve had offered to sit among the pines close to the dying
fire to keep watch for the first couple of hours. Then one
of the Alphonso Sebastian bunch would take over until
the first light of dawn.

But Steve wasn't a happy man. In fact he was far from
happy. What a damned fool I've been, he thought to
himself. Falling in with that madman is the worst thing I
ever did. A voice in his head kept whispering to him,
'Come tomorrow, you're going to get yourself killed, man.
And a poor living cowpuncher is a whole lot better than a
stiff corpse lying face up in the middle of Main Street in a

town called Silver Spur.' Steve wasn't the most imaginative of *hombres* but his imagination had worked overtime on this.

So when he supposed the rest of the bunch were snoring in their bedrolls, he saddled his horse and led it away from the camp and down towards the trail. He had no particular plan: he just wanted to get away from Black Bart and save his skin.

When it was time to relieve Steve, Pete stirred himself and walked towards where Steve should have been – but of course, Steve was nowhere to be seen. Pete was a cool dude and he didn't panic easily. So he checked the horses and concluded Steve had taken French leave. Pete considered his options. Do I wake Black Bart, or Alphonso Sebastian? he wondered. He decided on the latter.

He crept back stealthily until he found Alphonso. He bent and nudged Alphonso, 'Wake up, man,' he whispered.

Alphonso gave a snort. 'What's happening?' he asked, reaching for his wire-rimmed specs.

Pete bent closer. 'Steve's not here.'

'Not here! What do you mean, not here?'

'Keep your voice down, man.' Pete hissed. 'He's taken his horse and ridden off.'

Alphonso sat up and put on his specs. He peered around like an owl and focused on Pete. 'So Steve's jumped ship?' he said quietly.

'That seems to be the case,' Pete confirmed. 'He can't be far, but which way has he gone? That's the big question.'

CHAPTER NINE

The first faint streaks of dawn were shining in the east when Jack Kincade rose from his bed and dressed. He crept downstairs, put on his gunbelt, opened the door and looked out along Main Street. Bridget, his wife, said 'Why are you up so early?'

He put his finger to his lips: 'Don't wake the kids.'

Outside the air was fresh, and all he saw was a mangy dog limping across the street. He walked to the middle of Main Street and looked right and then left. Most of the town was still sleeping, but a few folks were already about their business. Then he stopped dead as he looked up the trail towards River Fork and saw a solitary rider moving steadily towards him. There was something about the guy that Jack Kincade found suspicious, something about the way the man rode – he kept stopping and glancing back to see whether he was being followed.

Jack stepped on to the sidewalk and stood still as a post as the rider rode towards him. As the man approached he jigged his horse forward as though he felt a little more confident.

Kincade drew his gun and stepped on to Main Street: 'Stop right there!' he called.

'Don't shoot!' the man cried tremulously.

'I won't shoot unless I have to. Why don't you get right down off your horse and come towards me. But don't come too close and don't make a false move, because I'm feeling a little high strung this morning and I'd hate to have to shoot a man unnecessarily.'

Steve held his arms in the air and said, 'I come in peace, sir. I'm looking for sanctuary.'

'Well, we don't have too much sanctuary here. So you'd better get down off your horse like I said, and unbuckle your gunbelt and let it fall because I'd hate to have to shoot you . . . before breakfast too.'

Steve dismounted and did as Jack Kincade ordered. As the gunbelt fell to the ground he looked back along Main Street in the direction of River Fork.

'So you think you're being followed?' Kincade said. 'Would that be Black Bart by any chance?'

Steve nodded. 'Bart's gone crazy as a loon. They're up there on the other side of the bluff, but they'll soon come down and I don't want to be part of it.'

'So you've just decided to convert from being a killer to a good honest citizen. Is that what you're telling me?'

Steve stepped on to the sidewalk keeping his hands in the air. 'I'm no yellow belly, Sheriff, and I'm no killer. I just came to warn you. I could have ridden to River Fork but I came here instead.'

'OK.' Kincade nodded and indicated the bench outside his office. 'Sit yourself down there and tell me about it.'

Steve shook his head. 'I can't say much, Sheriff, except they're coming down to rob the bank, and if I'm still here they'll shoot me down like a dog.'

'Then what do you suggest?' Kincade asked him.

Steve looked down at the sidewalk and then back along

119

the trail towards River Fork. 'I've told you all I know, Sheriff. Like, I don't want to hang and I don't want to be shot. Maybe I could hide out somewhere until the whole thing's over.'

'Just like a fairytale with a happy ending. But I'm going to have to lock you up in the town jail until after the winds of hell have blown through.'

'But that's the first place they'll look,' Steve protested.

'Not if they're dead!'

Jack Kincade wasn't as confident as he sounded. After he had locked Steve in the town jail behind his office, he stepped out on to the sidewalk and saw Adam Kirk looking down at Steve's discarded gunbelt.

'I saw what happened,' Kirk said. 'I was looking out of Bridget's window across the street. So you've locked up the guy in the town calaboose?'

'Only thing I could do.' Kincade told him what Steve had said about the impending raid.

'So, we need to get ready to face the music,' Kirk said.

Up on the other side of the bluff the whole bunch were up but Mart had no time to start breakfast since Black Bart was raving at him. 'Did you know about this?' he shouted with his enormous hand on Mart's throat.

'I didn't know a damned thing!' Mart protested. 'First I knew about it was when Pete sounded the alarm!'

'OK, Bartholomew,' Alphonso said, 'just try to keep calm. The man's gone and we have to decide on our next move.'

'That is so,' Jacob Merriweather agreed. 'Steve can't be far off. If he's down in Silver Spur, they'll be waiting for us. They might be getting a posse together to come up here and gun down on us right now.'

120

Black Bart stopped to consider. 'I don't think they could do that. We'd see them coming and we're in a strong position up here. That's why I chose the place.'

'So what do we do? Cut our losses and ride to some place else?' Alphonso asked.

Bart started pacing up and down like Napoleon before the Battle of Waterloo. Then he turned furiously. 'Well, I'm going down there even if I have to go alone. There's just a bunch of hicks down there and we can easily outgun them.'

'What about the sheriff?' someone asked.

Black Bart gave a snort. 'That sheriff couldn't shoot a sitting duck in a shooting gallery ten feet in front of his nose. He should have retired himself way back.'

'Yeah, and what about Adam Kirk? D'you think he's a pushover too?'

'Kirk ain't worth a silver nickel. He's no more than a boy who can't grow a beard on his face. I'll just ride down there and shoot him down dead.'

'Well, those are danged fine words,' Merriweather said, 'but we have to walk the walk and shoot the shoot if we go down there.'

'OK!' Black Bart roared, 'If you *hombres* haven't got the balls for the job Mart and me will do it on our own.'

'No need to get all riled up about it,' Alphonso protested.

'All right, all right!' Black Bart said. 'So what do you suggest?'

'What I suggest,' Alphonso said, 'is we ride into town by the back route and hit the bank while Kincade and Kirk are looking up the trail towards River Fork, or even better we could ride on and hit the trail on the other side of town and come in that way.'

Pete gave a low laugh. 'You think those two lawmen are dumb enough to stand staring towards River Fork like the folk in the Good Book staring up to Heaven while we hold up the bank?'

Alphonso adjusted his specs. 'It might not be quite as crazy as it sounds. We are six against two. Why don't we divide up in pairs? Two of us go directly for the bank, two of us cut into town on the other side of Main Street, and two of us hit the other end of town from the east. That way they won't know where we're coming from. They might even think we're the hordes of Midian.'

That reduced everyone to a stunned silence. Most of them hadn't a clue who the hordes of Midian were anyway.

'So who's doing what?' Black Bart asked.

Alphonso adjusted his specs yet again, as though seeing clearly helped him to reason things out more rationally. 'Why don't you and Mart do the bank. Jacob and Pete can cut in from the other side of Main Street, and me and Judd will ride in from the other end of town and engage the two lawmen, if necessary?'

The plan seemed to appeal to everyone, including Black Bart who was raring to break into the bank. He was already thinking of his future home in California, and he hadn't forgotten about Katie Smiley warming his slippers by the fire, either! 'Well, that's what I suggested in the first place,' he said smugly. 'And if we happen to meet that traitorous rattler Steve on the way I'm gonna hang him by his thumbs and shoot him full of holes!'

'That's what you think,' Mart said to himself.

In the back room of the Long Branch Saloon Katie was sitting with Kev's wife Sophia.

'So you'll be on the road to Missouri come sun-up?'

Sophia said.

Katie gave that open-hearted smile that appealed to everyone, particularly Adam Kirk. 'Pa wants to set up his own theatre group, which seems like a good idea. He has no head for business. So I need to give him all the help I can.'

Sophia gave her a secretive smile. 'You know Adam Kirk and Charlie the Medic rode into town the day before yesterday?'

Katie pursed her lips. 'I've been trying not to think about them. I have to make sure Pa doesn't get into any more scrapes, and I shan't be quiet in my mind until we get back to Missouri.'

'Well, that's quite a long ride and you've been a real support to your pa.' Sophia paused for a moment. 'But before you leave I have a gift for you.' She pushed a small bag across the table.

'Well, thank you, Sophia,' Katie said in surprise. 'What is it?'

'Open it carefully and look inside. I've had it since I was a girl and I've never had occasion to use it. In view of what's happened recently I thought I'd give it to you.'

Katie put her hand in the bag and felt a small metal object. She pulled it out and rested it in the palm of her hand.

'That's a Derringer single shot,' Sophia said, 'small enough to hide in your skirts but deadly enough to shoot any man who tries to molest you. It isn't loaded, but if you reach further down you'll find a box of cartridges. They're small but deadly at close range.'

Katie weighed the weapon in her hand.

'It's the easiest thing in the world to use,' Sophia told her. 'And by the Grace of God I've never had occasion to

123

use it. So now I want you to have it just in case you come across one of those ugly *hombres* who wants to harm you. So hide it away somewhere just in case you need it.'

Katie looked down at the deadly weapon in her hand and trembled with fear. 'Well, thank you, Sophia. I hope I never have to use it.'

Jack Kincade and Adam Kirk were sitting together under the overhang outside the sheriff's office when John Smiley appeared; they saw that he was wearing his gun on his hip.

'Good morning, gentlemen,' he greeted them. 'Mind if I sit down and join you?'

'Please yourself, Mr Smiley,' Kincade said.

John Smiley sat down beside Adam Kirk. 'Life is full of coincidences, isn't it, Adam?'

'Anything in particular you had in mind?' Adam asked.

'Well, it seems kind of strange that me and my girl come riding into town and then you and Charlie come riding in later. Like the magnets of Heaven are drawing us together. Have you thought about that, Adam?'

Kirk gave him a brief smile. 'Where is Miss Katie right now?' he asked.

'I think she's chewing hard on the fat with Kev's good lady Sophia. Sophia's always been one of our most enthusiastic supporters, and they get on just fine.'

Kirk nodded. 'So why are you carrying that hogleg on your hip?'

John Smiley gave one of his most disarming smiles. 'That's because you're going to need it some time soon.'

Jack Kincade was looking along the trail towards River Fork. He noted the town had gone as quiet as the grave just before a funeral service, but there was no music, not even the Dead March. Even the lame dog had taken cover.

Jack looked across Main Street and made sure that Bridget's Diner had the closed sign over the door, and he thought about the small town school and whether his kids were safe.

There was a heat haze shimmering at the end of Main Street, and through it he saw two riders jogging towards him; they were like spectres riding in from heaven or hell. The next second they had disappeared like smoke.

John Smiley was standing on the edge of the sidewalk when there was a shot and he lurched back with a gasp and fell.

Adam Kirk was on his feet immediately. The shot had come from the other side of Main Street in the vicinity of the bank. He crouched, drew his gun, and got ready to return fire. But there was no target.

He looked down at John Smiley and saw blood spurting from his shirt close to the shoulder. 'I've been hit!' Smiley gasped in astonishment.

Kirk and Kincade dragged him into Kincade's office and John Smiley groaned and passed out just as another shot sliced into the door jam.

'Where the hell did that come from?' Kincade said.

'Somewhere close by the bank. Take care of Smiley. I'll see if I can get a bead on them.' Kirk crouched and darted down the sidewalk towards Doc Buchanan's office and almost collided with Charlie the Medic. 'What are you doing here?' he gasped.

'I've just been with Doc Buchanan,' Charlie said. 'And I've come to warn you there's shooting going on behind the Long Branch Saloon. They're coming in from both directions.'

Both sides of Main Street, Kirk thought. 'Listen,' he said aloud. 'John Smiley's lying in the sheriff's office. He's

125

taken one in the shoulder and he's bleeding bad, so he needs your help. Go down there but don't get yourself shot on the way. Tell Kincade they're coming in from both sides of the street.'

'What will you do?' Charlie asked him.

'I'll do whatever I have to do.'

Charlie grunted and ran towards the sheriff's office just as fast as he could.

Thoughts were buzzing round Kirk's mind like killer wasps. 'Keep calm,' he said to himself aloud. 'Try to figure out what's happening and who's making it happen.' In his mind two thoughts were uppermost. The first was that someone was robbing the bank, and the second was that Katie Smiley might be in great danger if the gunmen were closing in on the Long Branch Saloon. I don't give a cuss about the money he thought, but I have to save that girl!

Yet even as he was thinking, instinct drove him on, and he fired a shot in the direction of the bank and darted across Main Street. He reached the other side and pressed himself against the wall of Bridget's Diner, just as Bridget herself threw open the door.

'Get yourself in here!' she yelled.

Kirk flung himself inside and bolted the door behind him. He suddenly knew what he must do. 'Get under cover and stay there!' he said.

'What are you going to do?' she asked him.

'Listen!' he yelled. 'Jack's OK, and someone's firing across Main Street. My guess is it's Black Bart. I'm going out through the back way. So bolt the door behind me and keep your fingers crossed and pray hard if you believe in the heavenly powers.'

Bridget nodded briskly and followed him through to

126

the back door. 'Good luck,' she said as she bolted the door behind him.

Black Bart was in the bank pointing his gun at the bodies lying face down on the floor, the assistant and three customers who were in the bank when the robbers broke in. Bart turned to the manager who was busy filling up a gunny sack with dollar bills.

'Don't hold back, man, or I'll blow your damned head off!'

'I'm doing my best.' Spalding wailed. 'But please don't kill anyone, sir!'

One of the men on the ground half raised his head and Black Bart kicked him hard in the groin. 'Keep yourself still and don't try anything tricky if you don't want a hole in your head!'

The man stifled a gasp and tried to keep as still as his quick breathing would allow.

'It's all in the sack,' Spalding whined, 'every last dollar! It's all there, sir, I promise you.'

Black Bart slung the sack over his shoulder and went to the door and turned. 'You lie still!' he snarled, 'and count to a hundred and twenty. If anyone moves an inch I'm coming right back to blast him to hell!'

'Yes, sir,' the manager stammered. 'Nobody's going to move, I promise you.'

Bart threw open the door and stepped out on to the sidewalk where Mart was crouching behind a barrel. 'Did you wing anyone?' Bart asked Mart.

'I scored one big time,' Mart said. 'Not sure who it was, but my guess would be it was that entertainer John Smiley. I don't think he'll be smiling much any more!'

'That was a good start.' Black Bart looked to the right

and saw two riders approaching. They were Alphonso and Judd and they were riding fast. Black Bart stepped off the sidewalk and raised his arm. He put the sack full of dollars on the edge of the sidewalk. 'Just in time for the big party!' he exclaimed.

Alphonso was looking down at the sack full of dollars. 'Looks like you cleaned out the bank, Bartholomew. Maybe we should get out of town while the going's good.'

Black Bart laughed triumphantly. 'Not yet, my friend! I have other fish to fry!'

Alphonso dismounted and kept his horse between him and the other side of Main Street. 'Are you serious, my friend?'

'Serious as hell!' Black Bart yelled. 'I'm going over there to blast hell out of that ornary John Smiley and make sure he's dead as rotting timber. Then I'm gonna shoot up whoever's in my path. Those critters don't know what's gonna hit them.'

Alphonso's mouth opened in astonishment and he glanced first at the sack of dollars and then at Judd, who gave a slight nod.

The back door of the bank was bolted, as Kirk had expected. So he edged along the side until he was facing Main Street, and peered out cautiously: he saw Mart and Black Bart and the other two. Fate was playing right into his hands: he could shoot the whole bunch down before they had time to react. But who would be first? Yet before he could make his move something unexpected happened. Judd, Alphonso's sidekick, suddenly drew his gun and levelled it at Black Bart, which was just what Bart had expected. He was big as a bear and twice as heavy, but he had the instincts of a rattlesnake and he fired a shot point black at Judd. Judd had never been heard to say much, but he screamed and leaped back against his horse and sank on to the dust of Main Street. His horse reared and kicked out as Black Bart sprang back against the door of the bank where he was out of sight to Kirk.

Then something else totally unexpected occurred: Mart fired a shot at Alphonso and missed. The shot hit Alphonso's horse in the rump. The horse screamed and galloped across Main Street where it collapsed and lay still.

Alphonso didn't stop to adjust his specs, but fired a shot directly at Mart, who fell back against the hard wall of the bank and slid to the ground, coughing out his life blood.

Alphonso then fired a shot at the door of the bank, but the door was closed and the shot just rocketed off the hard wood. But Alphonso wasn't intent on killing Black Bart: he bent down and grabbed the sack full of dollars. Then he looked for his horse, but seeing it was collapsed he started legging it for the other side of Main Street.

Kirk levelled his Colt Peacemaker and took a bead on the retreating figure of Alphonso. Silver Spur Main Street was very wide even for a Western town, but Kirk knew he could bring the man down, indeed should bring the man down, before he reached the other side of the street. So he steadied his gun with both hands – but before he could squeeze the trigger, a shot rang out from his right, and Alphonso sprawled forward on his face with a bullet in his back. The sack full of dollars fell to the ground, and green-backs burst out in all directions.

Black Bart ran to the edge of the sidewalk with his smoking gun. 'That's what you get for being a yellow-bellied traitor!' he yelled. Then he ran forwards and shot the dying man through the head. 'Take a present from me!' he shouted.

Then he started to scoop up the dollars and stuff them back into the sack.

Kirk stepped off the sidewalk and levelled his gun, but before he could fire, someone else appeared: it was his friend Jack Kincade.

Kincade aimed his gun at Black Bart, but Black Bart turned with his gun in his hand and fired a shot at the sheriff. Kincade sank down and rolled over on to his side. Black Bart cocked his gun and fired directly at Kincade's head – but Fate intervened. The gun clicked against an empty chamber – Black Bart had run out of shells.

Black Bart looked back and saw Kirk running towards him with his gun raised. But Kirk didn't fire because Black Bart was so close to Kincade that he might have hit the sheriff.

Black Bart grabbed the sack full of dollars and made off as fast as he could for the sidewalk on the other side of Main Street. Then he merged into the shadows and stopped to reload his gun. 'Well, I've blasted that damned sheriff,' he said to himself. 'And now I'm gonna blast hell out of that interfering boy marshal!'

CHAPTER TEN

Kirk bent over Jack Kincade and found to his relief that his friend had his eyes wide open and he was still gasping for breath. 'Where have you been hit?' Kirk asked him.

'I don't know,' Kincade groaned. 'Let me lie here while you get after that madman.'

Kirk looked towards where Black Bart must be concealed, just as another shot sent up a spurt of dust six feet away from him. Black Bart had moved further along the street, and Kirk heard him laughing to himself as he drew near to the Long Branch Saloon.

Kirk sprinted across Main Street and dived behind a barrel. Then he turned to see Kincade's wife Bridget running from Bridget's Diner towards her stricken husband and Doc Buchanan hurrying towards them from his office. Kirk knew instantly what his priority should be. So he headed immediately for the Long Branch Saloon, keeping under cover of the *ramada.*

Katie Smiley was in the back room of the Long Branch Saloon with Kev's wife Sophia when they heard the commotion; both leaped to their feet.

'There's shooting!' Sophia exclaimed. She made for the door to the bar but before she could open it the door

131

to the yard behind her was flung open and two armed men appeared. Both women put their hands to their mouths to stifle screams.

'What d'you want?' Sophia demanded despite her terror.

Jacob Merriweather was smiling, but she noted he was holding a gun held high against his shoulder. 'Don't alarm yourself unduly, dear lady,' he said. 'We just stepped inside for a moment to shelter from the storm, so to speak.'

His companion gave a somewhat sinister chuckle.

'Who are you?' Sophia demanded bravely.

Merriweather continued to smile. 'Just two strangers passing through, ma'm. So don't get unduly distressed. If you don't mind, we'll just pass through to the bar-room.'

Katie was standing close to the door to the bar-room. 'There's nothing for you in there,' she said. 'So why don't you just turn round and go right out through that door again?'

Merriweather looked down at her and smiled. 'You wouldn't be Katie Smiley, would you, pretty lady?'

'What's that to you?' Katie snapped.

Merriweather stepped forward and grabbed her by the chin none too gently. But instead of flinching or drawing away Katie stared right back into his eyes. 'Take your hands off me!' she demanded.

'Well, now . . .' Merriweather relinquished his hold on her chin. 'You sure have *cojones*, lady, which is somewhat unusual for the female of the species. Wouldn't you agree, Pete?'

Pete gave that edgy chuckle again.

Merriweather stepped back. 'Well, now, unless I'm mistaken you're that entertainer's girl. I heard you tapping those ivory keys up in River Fork, and you played like one

of those maestros they have across the wide water. No
wonder Bartholomew has taken such a shine to you.'

The mention of Black Bart made Katie wince, but she
wasn't about to show Merriweather her fear. 'That man is
nothing but a vicious brute!' she declared.

Merriweather was still smiling. 'I'm inclined to agree
with you on that, ma'am. Maybe he had a bad childhood.
But there we are. You have to live with what's handed out
to you. Now, if you'll be kind enough to step aside, I'll just
push through to the bar-room.'

Black Bart thrust open the double doors of the bar-
room and pushed his way in from Main Street. There were
very few men in the bar apart from Tiny Broadhurst and
Kev, the owner of the Long Branch Saloon. Kev was standing behind the bar and Tiny Broadhurst was half
crouching behind an upturned table.

Bart turned to Kev. 'Come right over to the doors and
bolt them up good and tight so nobody can get in.' He
waved his gun in Kev's direction. 'And do it pronto before
I blast your head off your shoulders.'

'Yes, sir.' Kev edged quickly round the bar, moved to the
double doors and threw the bolt across – but not before
he'd glanced through the window and seen Doc
Buchanan and Bridget Kincade tending the sheriff in the
middle of Main Street. 'You shot the sheriff!' he said to
Black Bart.

'He got what was coming to him!' Black Bart retorted.
'And that big mouth John Smiley got his, too!'

Kev had seen a few rough deals in his time, but he had
always tried to keep his cool; it was part of his stock in
trade. He could hear Tiny Broadhurst quietly shitting his
pants behind the table, but at that moment, he was thinking more about his wife Sophia and Katie Smiley in the

back room.

'OK,' Black Bart said, 'keep that door locked good and tight. If I hear so much as a mouse's fart, I'll come back in and shoot you so full of holes you'll look like that pepper pot you got on top of the bar. You hear me!'

'Yes, sir, we hear you!' Tiny Broadhurst wailed from behind his upturned table.

Black Bart hoisted the bag full of dollar bills on to his shoulder and made for the door to the back room.

Adam Kirk heard the bolts slide into place, so he knew he couldn't go into the Long Branch Saloon by the front way. So he edged back and made for the corner of the building. Then he stooped and ran towards the back, which was quite a stretch. When he reached the end of the passage, he flattened himself against the wall and peered cautiously right and left to see a familiar figure making his way towards him; it was his *compadre* Charlie the Medic.

Charlie ran forward and crouched beside him. 'I came to warn you,' he gasped. 'John Smiley's been hit.'

'How bad?' Kirk asked.

'Bad enough,' Charlie said, 'but the chances are he'll survive. All hell's breaking loose out there. Jack Kincade's lying on Main Street, and he might be dead. The whole world's gone crazy! D'you know where that big bag of shit Black Bart is?'

Kirk moved his head to the right. 'He's inside the Long Branch and they've locked the front door.'

'So that's why you're here?' Charlie said.

Kirk bent low and peeked round the corner towards the back entrance of the Long Branch Saloon. The area was full of trash cans and other debris from the saloon. 'The trouble is I think Katie Smiley's in there too!'

'That's bad news!' Charlie said. 'So what do we do?'

Kirk didn't answer. Charlie never carried a gun, so it was just him against Black Bart, and Bart held all the aces.

Black Bart threw open the door to the back room, thrust out his gun, and came face to face with Jacob Merriweather who was pointing a gun at him. A little to the left of Merriweather Pete half crouched with his gun, also trained on Black Bart. The two women were on the right and both were staring at Bart wide-eyed and terrified.

'Well, now,' Merriweather said in a surprisingly calm tone. 'So I see you got your sack full of dollars, Bartholomew.' He gestured towards the sack on the floor in the doorway. 'What happened to Alphonso?'

Bart gave a sneer, but his gun didn't waver. 'He's lying stiff on Main Street on account of he got a little too greedy.'

Merriweather nodded. 'Greed is a terrible vice, Bartholomew. So what's our next move?'

'Our next move is we go out through that door behind you and get clean away with the dollars.'

'Except we only have two horses,' Pete put in.

'Well, that could be something of a difficulty,' Merriweather agreed.

Merriweather and Bart exchanged wary glances.

Black Bart shrugged. 'There's plenty of horses in town.'

Merriweather gestured towards the back door. 'You go out through that door you're likely to get a slug in your brain.'

Black Bart shook his head. 'I don't think so 'cause I'm taking the Smiley girl along with me and if that boy soldier's around he won't want to see her bleeding and dead.'

Merriweather grinned. 'And what about those precious dollars?'

Black Bart showed his rotting teeth. 'You'll get your share of the dollars and I get my share plus the girl.'

Merriweather nodded. 'OK, that's a deal, just as long as you're straight down the line with me.'

'Nothing could be straighter.' Bart gestured with his gun towards Katie. 'Come over here, girl. This is where your future begins.'

Katie looked at Sophia and nodded. Sophia looked right back at her and she was close to tears.

Merriweather smiled. 'I'm sorry to trouble you,' he said to Sophia. 'We're in some difficulty here. So I guess you should come along too. Just for insurance purposes, you understand,' he added.

Adam Kirk was still trying to figure out what to do when the back door of the Long Branch Saloon was thrust open and Katie Smiley stepped out, followed closely by Black Bart with a gun held to her head. Kirk was ready to shoot Black Bart dead but, as he cocked his revolver, Bart swung Katie towards him and shouted, 'Don't shoot unless you want to kill this fine lady!'

Kirk lowered his gun. 'I'm not going to shoot,' he said, 'just as long as you let Miss Smiley go and walk away from her.'

Bart gave a low growl of laughter. 'That ain't part of the deal, sir. Katie Smiley is coming with me and we're gonna ride right out of town together.'

Katie was looking at Kirk and he saw terror in her eyes. He lowered his gun.

The next moment Sophia stepped out of the door with Merriweather close behind her and he had a gun pressed to her back.

'Don't fret yourself unduly, Mr Kirk,' he said in a some-what lighter tone. 'No harm will come to these ladies just

136

as long as you do as you're bid.'

Then Pete appeared close behind Merriweather.

'So what is your bidding?' Kirk asked Merriweather.

Merriweather shrugged. 'Just our horses, Mr Kirk. That's all we ask. Give us half an hour and we'll bother you no more.'

Kirk saw he didn't have much choice. He switched to Black Bart. 'If any harm comes to that young lady, I'll kill you stone dead if I have to ride from hell and back to do it.' But his voice wasn't as firm as he had intended.

Black Bart gave a growl of laughter: 'Don't you worry, Soldier Boy! Miss Smiley's mine for ever now and there ain't nothing you can do about it. I'm taking her with me to the end of the wide world and back. So I hope you've got a picture of her 'cause that's all you're getting, Soldier Boy.'

'*Miss Smiley's mine for ever now and there ain't nothing you can do about it.*' Those blood-chilling words ricocheted in Kirk's mind like bullets hitting a corrugated iron wall. He looked at Katie and she stared back at him. No words passed between them but their eyes spoke volumes. Yet there wasn't a thing they could do . . . for the moment.

Pete went off in search of horses and he seemed to be gone for so long that Kirk began to think the man had cut and run. Black Bart and Jacob Merriweather had pulled the two women back into the doorway, and for a while nobody spoke.

Kirk looked at the two men and tried to read their faces. Black Bart's face didn't need a lot of reading. He was chuckling triumphantly to himself and speaking into Katie Smiley's ear. 'Don't you worry none, pretty lady. We're gonna have a great time together in California where the sun shines bright every day.'

Jacob Merriweather, on the other hand, had an unread-able look on his face as though he wasn't too pleased about holding his gun to Sophia's back. Kirk noticed that he kept glancing at Bart and then down at the sack full of dollars at the man's feet. That's all the guy cares about, Kirk thought. If he could get his hands on those green-backs, he'd be happy to ride off into the sunset on his own.

Then Pete rode in on the horses, leading an extra one.

'So you got three hosses,' Black Bart grinned again.

'There's mine and Jake's and with a little persuasion I managed to borrow one more with a saddle and all.'

'My hoss is over back of the bank,' Bart said, 'but I don't care to go over there right now in case I meet a spook or two.' He grabbed Katie's arm. 'I'm gonna mount that bronco and pull you up so we can sit cosy together, and practise for the future.' He turned to Merriweather. 'Keep your gun on this soldier boy while me and the girl mount up. Then you mount up and we ride out of town by the back route, you hear me.'

Adam Kirk and Charlie the Medic watched with a degree of horror as Black Bart mounted his horse and pulled Katie up in front of him. Kirk couldn't do a thing to stop him; he knew if he made a move Katie would be shot dead on her horse or hurled to the ground. Then something happened that surprised him. Jacob Merriweather pushed Sophia to one side and said, 'OK, pretty lady, you've played your part. Now you can go back to your husband and take a drink to celebrate your freedom.'

'What about Miss Smiley?' Sophia asked.

'She comes with me,' Black Bart shouted. 'And remem-ber, Soldier Boy, if you ride after us, the first to drop will be this good lady – but I guess you won't be dumb enough

138

to do that, will you?'

After that they rode away out of town.

Horror was etched on Charlie's face. 'What do we do now, *mon ami*?'

'There's only one thing we can do,' Kirk replied. 'I find my horse and ride after those sons of bitches, and you go back to your patients and make sure they stay alive.'

'But . . .'

'There's no "but" about it.' Kirk holstered his gun and ran as fast as he could to where his horse was tethered.

Black Bart was riding along the trail to River Fork with Katie Smiley riding in front of him. It might have looked cosy, but to Katie it felt like riding with a devil from the lowest circle of hell. Jacob Merriweather and Pete were scouting ahead, *keeping an eye out for trouble* as Bart had instructed. The real reason, as Merriweather understood, was not so much the scouting ahead, but the fact that Bart didn't trust a living soul, specially when a sack full of dollars was concerned.

Merriweather had never been a covetous man. He was an outlaw because of an irrepressible sense of adventure and a hatred of all authority. *Don't fence me in* was his favourite phrase. But as they jogged along he glanced to his left and saw the sack full of dollars between Katie and Black Bart, and strange thoughts started to take shape in his mind, and he looked at Black Bart with growing distaste. 'That greasy shit killed my friend Alphonso,' he thought, 'though Alphonso should have seen it coming a mile away, even through those wire-rimmed specs of his that are probably now lying twisted and broken on Silver Spur Main Street.'

Then he looked across at Katie Smiley and thought,

'That young woman has real style and taste. And I hate to see a woman abused by a brute like Bart; it offends my sense of what is the right way to treat womenfolk.'

Then his mind turned to the sack full of dollars again, and he started thinking about what he should do to get his hands on them.

Kirk was off the trail, riding through higher country; looking down through the cottonwood trees he saw Black Bart and Merriweather, and Pete leaving the trail and pushing off to the left.

Kirk knew the trail pretty well and he guessed they were headed for the bluff not far from Silver Spur where they could look down and scan the trail and feel safe. So Kirk guided his mount down towards the trail and considered his tactics.

'Where do we make camp?' Merriweather asked Bart.

'Just as far way from Silver Spur as we can,' Bart replied.

'Well, don't leave it too late,' Merriweather said, glancing at Pete.

Pete looked down and said nothing.

'Don't you boys worry none. I know just the place,' Bart said.

Merriweather observed: 'By my reckoning with our haul from the two bank jobs you could divvy it out when we make camp and then we could take our share and go our separate ways.'

'That sounds like good sense to me,' Pete said. 'That way it will put confusion on anyone trying to track us.'

Black Bart laughed. 'If you're thinking of that boy soldier,' he said, 'forget it. All he's got between his pink little ears is love songs and the cooing of doves. That boy doesn't even know he's born yet.'

'That's not what I heard,' Pete said, glancing at Merriweather.

'Well, you heard a load of horse shit,' Black Bart said. 'If that boy tracks down on us he won't know what hit him till he bites the dust, and that will be just a bit too late.' And Bart roared with laughter at his own wit!

Katie didn't need to listen. She could feel Bart's foul breath on the back of her neck.

'I've had a thought,' Black Bart said. 'There's a place a little up yonder between two bluffs.'

'I think I know where you mean,' Pete said.

'Well, then,' Bart said, 'why don't we split up and lay a trap for that boy soldier. Then we can shoot him down and pass on our way.'

'You mean after we've divided up the dollars?' Merriweather said.

Black Bart gave his growling laugh again. 'You mean you don't trust me, Jake?'

'Trust among thieves. Isn't that what they say?' Pete said.

'That's just an old story for women and dried up old men,' Bart retorted. 'So what do you think?'

Neither Jacob Merriweather nor Pete replied. They were drawing close to the narrow defile that Bart had in mind.

'OK,' Merriweather said after a moment, 'Pete and me will go up here to the right, and when your boy soldier comes riding through we'll gun down on him.'

'Except he might not be alone. There could be a whole posse of them,' Pete said realistically.

'Better still. We could pick them off as they ride down the defile, easy as shooting clay pigeons at a fair,' Black

141

Bart returned.

Bart spurred his mount forward up the bluff on the left, but the hill was steep and the horse Pete had taken was old and weak, and Bart knew it would take a century to get to the top of the bluff. So he said to Katie, 'Listen, girl, you know how to walk, 'cause we're gonna have to get off this bony old nag and lead it up to the top of the bluff.' He swung his leg off his mount and plumped himself down on the ground. 'Get down off that hoss and don't get any ideas in case I have to shoot you, d'you hear me?'

'I hear you,' Katie replied. But as she leaped down from the horse her mind was racing ahead.

'Now walk in front of me,' Black Bart commanded, 'and when we get to the top of the bluff you do as I say and you'll live long enough to see that boy soldier of yourn drop dead in his boots.'

'That's what you think,' Katie said to herself.

Jacob Merriweather and Pete were on the ridge of the other bluff, from where they could look down at the defile and also across to the other bluff where Black Bart would be lying looking down at the trail.

'You think this is the best move?' Pete asked.

'I think it's the only move,' Merriweather replied. 'If Adam Kirk is fool enough to ride down that trail, he might just as well be putting his head in a noose and I don't think he's fool enough for that.'

'Then what are you thinking to do in that giant brain of yours, Jacob?'

Merriweather smiled and nodded. 'I haven't figured it out yet, my friend, but I'll tell you one thing. I couldn't stand the stink of that *hombre* a moment longer. And seeing the way he's treating that girl was making me sick to my stomach.'

Pete nodded. 'Well, that's not the best of reasons, is it? What we need to do is get our hands on that sack of dollars. The rest doesn't matter a two-bit piece.'

'Well, that's true, my friend, and that's what we're going to do.'

Kirk wasn't that far behind them. His trailing skills weren't as good as some of his First Nation friends, but he knew time wasn't on his side. So what could he do to rescue Katie Smiley from the clutches of that crazed killer?

He dismounted and studied the signs. There was no doubt the bunch had come this way – the horse apples told him as much. Then he took the reins and led his mount forwards, stooping for time to time to examine the signs. 'Don't hurry!' he murmured to himself. 'A man who hurries is a man who's likely to get himself killed. And that won't help Katie Smiley, will it?' Then he stopped and knelt down and looked at the tracks again, and suddenly realized that his tracking skills were somewhat better than he had thought. He saw that the tracks divided, and one horse was somewhat heavier than the other two, and the heavier horse had turned towards the left while the other two had gone right towards the other bluff.

'Well, now, my friend,' he said to his horse. 'If we're going to rescue that sweet young lady we have to follow the trail to the left. But take it easy, son, because that poor young woman is in real trouble.'

He urged his horse forwards, stopping to read the signs every few yards. His mind was working overtime and he saw that the horse bearing Bart and Katie was tiring. Then he saw the footprints and knew they had dismounted and walked on towards the top of the ridge.

'OK,' he said more to himself than the horse. 'You bide here for a spell while I go alone to the ridge.'

Black Bart ordered Katie to lie down at the edge of the bluff just ahead of him so that he could keep an eye on her and look down on the trail. 'You do as I say, girl, and you'll soon be enjoying the high life in California. But don't think of calling out or making a wrong move or you'll be lying here waiting for the coyotes to lick your bones dry.' Then he got up on to his knees and peered down at the trail below. After that he stared across at the other bluff where Jacob Merriweather and Pete would be waiting. And Merriweather waved across to him.

Black Bart wasn't the brightest spark in the West, but he soon realized that Adam Kirk was nowhere on the trail. He had either given up or was somewhere else entirely. Bart stood up and turned round. 'Get up, girl!' he commanded.

But Katie was already half way to her feet, and when she rose, Black Bart saw she was holding a small Derringer and pointing it right at him. 'What the hell!' he growled. 'Give that toy to me!' He stretched out his hand to take the gun, but as he reached for it Katie jerked the trigger and there was a sharp explosion. Katie sprang back in alarm. She had never fired a gun before, and had never wanted to, so she had aimed low and the bullet struck Black Bart in his right inner thigh just below the crutch.

'What the hell!' he roared again, before his leg gave way and he fell.

Katie had dropped the Derringer and fallen on to her back.

'Why you. . . !' Black Bart struggled to get to his feet. Then he looked down and saw the blood spreading over

144

the front of his pants. 'You hit me in the balls!' he roared. 'I'm gonna kill you for that!' He groped around for his Colt, but a foot came out and kicked it away. He looked up and saw Kirk standing above him with a gun pointed at his head.

Then that great hulk of flesh just passed out and fell with a groan.

Kirk picked up Black Bart's revolver and stuck it though his belt. Then he turned to Katie and stretched out his hand to help her to her feet.

'What happened?' she gasped.

'You just shot a man,' Kirk told her.

'Did I kill him?'

Kirk shook his head. 'I guess he'll live long enough to meet the hangman.'

Katie burst into tears and fell into Kirk's arms.

'This isn't exactly the right time,' he said quietly, 'but could the answer be yes?'

'Yes,' she whispered, and then more strongly, 'Yes!'

CHAPTER ELEVEN

Merriweather was looking across the ravine through his spyglass when he heard the shot and saw Black Bart stagger back and fall.

'That girl shot Bart!' he exclaimed.

Pete laughed; he'd seen it with his own eyes. 'Well, he deserved it, didn't he? Can't say I'd shed too many tears over that great hulk of blubber. That young lady sure has grit! She deserves some sort of medal!'

'Look now!' Merriweather exclaimed. 'I see someone else over there, and unless I'm going blind that must be that boy soldier Bart keeps on talking about.' He passed the spyglass to Pete.

Pete focused the spyglass. 'That's no boy soldier,' he said. 'That there is Marshal Adam Kirk, and he isn't the fool that Bart takes him to be.' He handed the spyglass back and Merriweather refocused it.

'It seems Bart isn't quite dead yet. They're getting him up on his feet, but it isn't easy. I can hear him moaning and groaning even from here.'

Merriweather and Pete laughed.

*

Kirk had his gun on Black Bart, and he wasn't taking any chances.

'Why don't you go and get that horse and bring him here so we can get this bundle of horse apples into the saddle?' he said to Katie.

Black Bart was supporting himself against a sapling. 'I can't ride!' he protested. 'How the hell am I gonna climb up into the saddle with this wounded leg? Can't you see I'm bleeding to death!'

'Well, the way I look at it, you don't have a lot of choice.' Kirk prodded him with his Peacemaker. 'Either you get on that horse and risk bleeding to death, or you lie here and wait for the coyotes or the wolves or even a passing grizzly to get you. So which do you prefer?'

Katie appeared leading the big horse. She was still shaking.

Kirk gave her a wry grin. 'Well now, Miss Katie Smiley, I'm afraid we only have the two horses, and the one picked out for this bag of horse manure is a little too weak to carry two people, so I guess you'll have to ride with me. I hope you don't mind that?'

Katie might have blushed in different circumstances, but now she merely smiled.

Kirk manoeuvred the weary nag towards Black Bart. 'Now, get yourself up on this poor broken bag of bones,' he said to Bart. 'You can use that sapling to hoist yourself up.'

'How the hell can I do that?' Black Bart complained.

'Well, like I said, either you wait here to be eaten by wolves or you climb up on that horse. So which do you prefer?'

Black Bart growled again but he saw that Kirk meant every word, so he grabbed the saddle horn with one hand

and the sapling with the other and managed to get himself high enough to hoist his left leg over the horse's back. Then he groaned and looked down at his wounded leg. 'Look, I'm bleeding again,' he complained.

'I guess that poor horse won't worry too much about that,' Kirk said without sympathy. 'Now just take up the reins and ride slowly ahead of us down the bluff towards the trail. You hear me?'

'I hear you,' Black Bart replied.

'And one false move and you'll have a hole in your back to complement the one in your leg.'

Bart didn't reply; he was too busy reaching for the reins and trying to stifle his groans.

Jacob Merriweather was still watching through his spyglass. He couldn't hear what was being said and he couldn't see everything because of the intervening foliage, but he could see enough to set his imagination buzzing. 'Well, I'll be damned!' he exclaimed.

'Let me take a looksee,' Pete said.

'You don't need to look,' Merriweather said. 'This isn't a peep show. So I'll just fill you in on the details. That hulk has got himself up into the saddle, and my guess is they're riding down the bluff towards the trail.'

'Did you see the sack of dollars, my friend?'

'I neither saw them nor smelled them,' Merriweather said.

'So what do we do?' Pete asked him.

'Well, the first thing we do is we grab our horses and mount up.'

'You know what,' Pete said, 'those dollars are within easy reach.'

'How do you figure that, my friend?

'What I figure is we ride down towards the trail and come in on them from behind.'

'You mean just shoot them down?' Merriweather asked.

'Why not?' Pete said. 'This is a mighty rough world and there's a hell of a lot of dollars in that sack.'

Merriweather raised an eyebrow. 'Are you telling me you would shoot Adam Kirk and that girl performer in the back for a sack full of dollars?'

Pete looked perplexed. 'Why else would we be here?'

Merriweather considered for a moment. 'When I rode out West I wanted to be free from the law and everything that tied me in. And then I fell in with Alphonso and we got on together like brothers. Then we met Bart and he was a real pig of a man . . . a man who would shoot his grandmother for just a few dollars. And now he's going to swing, and I don't want to swing with him.'

'Well, thanks for the sermon, my friend, but what does this add up to?'

Merriweather turned to scrutinize him. 'What it adds up to is this. I've come to the conclusion that those dollars don't mean a thing to me. So I'm not aiming to kill for them, especially when it comes to that brave young woman.'

'So . . .' Pete chuckled . . . 'you've taken a real shine to her?'

Merriweather grinned. 'No, I've just become a little more human, that's all.'

'So, what does that mean exactly?'

'It means I'm going to ride away from the scene.'

'What about me?' Pete asked.

Merriweather raised his eyebrow again. 'Well, my friend, you must do exactly what you want to do. But I hope you don't harm that brave young woman because

149

she deserves to live.'

They mounted up and Merriweather stretched out his hand. '*Adios*, my friend. Ride well.'

Pete took his hand and pressed it tight. 'See you in wherever we end up.'

So Jacob Merriweather rode to the right, and Pete turned to descend towards the trail.

Kirk was in something of a quandary. He knew that Merriweather and Pete must be on the other hill, so when they reached the trail he and Katie would be horribly exposed. But he couldn't leave Katie to deal with Bart on her own. Bart might be wounded, but a cornered rat can be dangerous and a man facing the probability of the hangman's noose would be desperate to survive. So what should he do?

'Listen, Miss Katie,' he said quietly, 'we're not out of danger yet. Merriweather and the guy called Pete are still on the loose and they want those dollars badly.'

Katie nodded in agreement. 'So what do you suggest we do?'

'We have to outsmart them. If we ride straight down to the trail they're likely to come on us from behind.'

'So we wait behind a stand of trees until we see them?' she said.

They had almost reached the trail. 'OK, this is where we wait,' Kirk said. He turned to Bart. 'Rein in here and stay right in the saddle and don't make a sound, because if you do, I'm afraid I'll have to shoot you.'

Bart reined in and drooped forward, giving the impression he was faint through loss of blood.

Kirk dismounted and helped Katie down. He drew Bart's Colt from under his belt and held it out to Katie by the barrel. 'I want you to take this for your own protection. I hope you won't need it, but if you do, make a clean job of it. D'you think you can manage that?'

Katie looked down at the weapon and nodded. 'Look out for yourself,' she said.

Kirk knelt and covered the trail with his own gun.

Pete rode down the hill towards the trail, and as he rode he thought of Jacob Merriweather's parting words, 'I've just become a little more human.' But then he remembered that sack full of dollars. If he got his hands on those dollars he wouldn't need to share them with anyone. They'd be like the pot of gold at the end of the rainbow, to spend as he wished.

When he reached the trail he couldn't see a living soul. So he reined in and drew his gun. 'What the hell!' he thought.

A voice came from the other side of the trail. 'Why don't you just drop that gun?' it said.

Pete held his gun steady and looked across the trail and saw Kirk standing behind a tree. 'You want me to shoot you?' Pete said.

'No,' Kirk said, 'I want you to throw that gun on the trail and step forward with your hands in the air.'

Pete took a deep breath. 'I don't think I can do that.' He aimed at the figure standing among the trees. But Kirk held his gun out straight with both hands and squeezed the trigger. Pete didn't hear the explosion because he was dead before he hit the ground.

Charlie the Medic was standing on Main Street when he saw Kirk and Katie and Black Bart riding towards him. Katie was on Kirk's horse and Kirk was riding a strange horse that Charlie later identified as Pete's. He saw that

Bart was drooping low in the saddle as though he was asleep or possibly dead or dying.

As the party drew rein in front of Doc Buchanan's office, Charlie looked up at his friend.

'Thank God, you're still alive, Adam! How did you manage it?'

Kirk smiled down at him. 'More by luck than judgement,' he said, 'and with a lot of help from a very brave young lady.' He dismounted and helped Katie Smiley to the ground.

'How's my pa?' she asked.

'Your pa's as well as can be expected,' Charlie said, 'considering he took a bullet in his chest. But I guess he won't be doing a lot of entertaining in the near future.'

'I must see him,' Katie said.

Charlie pointed in the direction of Doc Buchanan's office. 'He's over in there with Jack Kincade.'

'So Jack's alive too,' Kirk said.

Charlie nodded. 'Took one in the shoulder. Luckily it didn't touch the lung, so we think he'll live.' Charlie looked at Black Bart, who seemed to be sliding out of the saddle towards the ground. 'So this is the great killer,' Charlie said.

Bart raised his head and said, 'I'm hit real bad right here in the balls and I'm like to bleed to death. Can someone help me?' His voice was at least an octave higher than usual.

Kirk said, 'Swing off to the left so you can support your weight on your left leg, and we'll get you into the doc's office so he can look at that wound.'

Bart grimaced. 'Why don't you just shoot me?' he said.

'Well, I'd be happy to oblige, but I don't think that's strictly within the law.'

They got Black Bart down from his horse and into Doc Buchanan's office with considerable difficulty. As he hobbled on to the sidewalk, people appeared from everywhere. 'That's Black Bart!' someone exclaimed. 'Are you gonna string him up?' another man asked.

Doc Buchanan appeared at the door. 'So this is the brave *hombre* who tried to kill my friend Jack!' he said. 'Well now, let's take a look at that leg.'

Black Bart hobbled up to the door and they manoeuvred him into the doc's office, behind which was a small room that served as a hospital ward where Jack Kincade and John Smiley lay in their beds. Both were awake and both had had bullets dug out of their wounds. Bridget Kincade was at her husband's side, and Katie was kneeling beside her father's bed.

Nobody looked especially happy to see the new arrival, but Black Bart was too busy keening and blaspheming about his wounded leg to notice. He hobbled with help behind a screen where Doc Buchanan examined his wound.

Doc Buchanan had no liking for killers but he was a professional healer so he treated Bart as he would have treated any other patient.

'Can you save my leg?' Bart whinned.

'Just as long as we can get that bullet out,' Doc Buchanan told him, 'And if you're worried about your manhood, there's just a little singeing about the groin. Nothing more. Not that you're likely to need it much where you're going.'

It was time to visit the funeral director. Adam Kirk left Katie Smiley with her pa and went to look at the dead men. Alphonso and Judd and Mart were lying in pine coffins side by side with their arms folded across their chests. They looked almost as pious as monks in prayer. The funeral director had even perched Alphonso's specs on his nose, slightly askew so that he had a scholarly air about him. Judd, on the other hand, looked faintly surprised as though someone had interrupted him in mid prayer, and Mart looked somewhat disconcerted and outraged.

'Almost look like saints, don't they?' the funeral director said to Kirk.

'Saints with blood red halos!' Kirk replied.

'Well, we've all got a few spots of blood on our hands,' the funeral director said. 'It's part of the human condition.'

Kirk gave a sardonic nod. 'Well, come sun-up tomorrow someone has to ride out and pick up another saintly gunslinger on the trail somewhere between here and River Fork – that's if the wolves haven't carried him off to hell during the night.'

Next Kirk went to the jail house behind Jack Kincade's office. The prisoner Steve was sitting on his bunk looking somewhat nervous.

'What happened?' he asked Kirk.

'What happened is your compadres are mostly dead.' Kirk gave him a detailed account of the dead men. 'So you see, my friend, you did the right thing, and that might just save your neck unless we can find some other reason to string you up.'

'I ain't never killed a man in my life,' Steve affirmed.

Kirk nodded. 'I think you'll need to convince the judge about that.'

'So what happened to Bart?' Steve asked.

Kirk grinned. 'He's been shot quite close to the *cojones* by a very fine young woman. Right where he deserves it.

Doc Buchanan's patching him up right now so he's fit to climb up the steps to the scaffold.'

The prisoner looked kind of thoughtful for a moment. 'What about Jake Merriweather? Is he with the funeral director too?'

Kirk shook his head, 'I'm afraid I can't account for Merriweather. He just rode off into the sunset. Maybe he had better thoughts about the dollars, which by the way are back in the bank, which pleases the manager a whole lot. They're counting the dollars right now.'

Kirk then went to the Long Branch Saloon to talk to Kev Stanley and his wife Sophia. When Kev saw him he reached for his best whiskey. 'So you finally got that killer?' Kev said.

'Katie Smiley got him with that Derringer Sophia provided. I just brought him in.'

Sophia appeared from the back room. 'I heard what happened,' she said. 'How is Katie?'

'She's with her pa right now. It looks like he's going to be OK. Doc Buchanan and my friend Charlie are looking after him really well.'

'Thank God for that!' Sophia exclaimed.

'And where is Tiny Broadhurst?' Kirk was looking round the bar-room, Tiny's second home.

'Tiny's at home,' Kev said.

'That's news to me; I didn't know he had a home.'

Kev grinned and Sophia laughed. 'Says he has a touch of fever on account of he didn't get a shot in at Black Bart. He wanted to claim the reward,' Sophia said.

Kirk walked back along Main Street feeling slightly uncertain about life. As he reached Doc Buchanan's office, he paused and wondered whether to go in. 'What am I doing here?' he thought. The door opened and his friend Charlie the Medic appeared.

'How are things in there?' Kirk asked him.

Charlie shrugged and held his head on one side. 'Well, Doc Buchanan did a really good job. He got that slug out of Black Bart's leg with no difficulty at all. I couldn't have done better myself.' He gave Kirk a sly look. 'But I guess you're not here for that, are you?'

Kirk smiled, 'Is she still in there?'

'Sure, she's been talking to her pa and I heard your name mentioned more than once.'

At that moment Katie Smiley appeared. She looked at Kirk and then at Charlie.

Charlie nodded. 'I think I'll just step across the street and speak with Bridget, reassure her that Jack is going to be OK.'

They watched Charlie stride across Main Street and then turned to one another.

'Did you mean it?' Kirk asked her.

'Did I mean what?' she asked.

Kirk couldn't stop smiling. 'Up there after you shot that killer, you said "yes" three times – or was it four? Now we're back in town I have to ask you again, did you mean it?'

They were standing close together looking into one another's eyes.

'Yes, I meant it,' she said, 'of course I meant it.'

Then right there on the sidewalk they kissed, and their kiss lasted a very long time.

Black Bart's leg healed well enough for him to go to trial six weeks later. Of course he pleaded not guilty, but the judge and the jury found him guilty, and the judge sentenced him to death by hanging. When the day came he climbed up the steps to the scaffold and looked at the assembled crowd. The hangman looped the rope over his head and tightened the noose. Someone in the crowd shouted, 'You dirty, rotten, stinking killer!' and Bart opened his mouth to reply. But it was too late: the hangman sprang the trapdoor and Bart dropped like a stone. He gave a violent kick and his head dropped forwards. Black Bart the killer was dead.

Neither Adam Kirk nor Jack Kincade was there to witness the execution. Jack was in Bridget's Diner with his wife and children, and Adam Kirk was with Katie and her father John Smiley.

The Kirk/Smiley wedding was a simple affair. Sophia had made a wedding dress for Katie, and everyone said the bride looked radiant. Though Kirk felt like a stuffed dummy in fine clothes, he looked smart enough to be in a waxworks museum, apart from his face, which was beaming like the sun on a fine summer's day!

After the ceremony the bride, contrary to tradition, played the piano herself, and her father, though he still had his arm in a sling, sang a song. There was great applause and a few speeches with ribald jokes, at which the guests laughed heartily.

A week later John Smiley and Katie headed east for their farm in Missouri, and naturally Adam Kirk rode with them. He had decided to resign as a US marshal, though nobody, least of all his wife Katie, expected him to settle down on the farm. He was too much of a wild mustang for that! Yet he was eager to help John Smiley set up his theatre group in the barn, and he found that he had a talent for building and administration too! When later the children appeared he had good reason to stay at home, and to his own and everyone's surprise he started writing about his experiences as a US marshal. And, what was even more surprising ... he found his readers enjoyed his writing and demanded more. So when he wasn't working in the theatre, he wrote with growing skill and increasing success.

After his narrow escape, Jack Kincade handed in his badge of office and retired as sheriff, much to Bridget's satisfaction. He grew somewhat stouter serving customers and yarning with folks in Bridget's Diner. He kept in touch with Adam Kirk, and even checked one or two of the ex-marshal's stories. Occasionally he would read one out to the diners, who would be amazed! After all, the world moves on and each generation has its own problems and its own solutions.

Charlie the Medic stayed on with Doc Buchanan for a while, and then, on the doc's recommendation, returned to medical school to complete his training. But he never forgot his friend Adam Kirk, and he became a regular visitor to the Missouri farm and theatre well into old age.

Jacob Merriweather didn't quite disappear into the sunset! In fact he became a respected citizen in Oregon. He was never rich, but he never regretted giving up that sack full of dollars in the town of Silver Spur!